Secrets

Storie

Select

by

Marthe Jocelyn

J808.83 J583
Jocelyn, Marthe.
Secrets

MID-CONTINENT PUBLIC LIBRARY
Liberty Branch
1000 Kent Street
Liberty, MO 64068

LI

Tundra Books

This collection copyright © 2005 by Marthe Jocelyn
Stories copyright © 2005 by the individual authors

Published in Canada by Tundra Books,
481 University Avenue, Toronto, Ontario M5G 2E9

Published in the United States by Tundra Books of Northern New York,
P.O. Box 1030, Plattsburgh, New York 12901

Library of Congress Control Number: 2004117242

All rights reserved. The use of any part of this publication
reproduced, transmitted in any form or by any means, electronic,
mechanical, photocopying, recording, or otherwise, or stored in a
retrieval system, without the prior written consent of the publisher –
or, in case of photocopying or other reprographic copying, a licence
from the Canadian Copyright Licensing Agency – is an
infringement of the copyright law.

Library and Archives Canada Cataloguing in Publication

Secrets : stories / selected by Marthe Jocelyn.

ISBN 0-88776-723-0

1. Short stories, Canadian (English).   2. Short stories, American.
I. Jocelyn, Marthe

PS8321.S393 2005   C813'.010806   C2004-907138-6

We acknowledge the financial support of the
Government of Canada through the Book
Publishing Industry Development Program
(BPIDP) and that of the Government of Ontario
through the Ontario Media Development
Corporation's Ontario Book Initiative. We
further acknowledge the support of the Canada Council for the
Arts and the Ontario Arts Council for our publishing program.

ONTARIO ARTS COUNCIL
CONSEIL DES ARTS DE L'ONTARIO

Design: Cindy Reichle

Printed in Canada

1 2 3 4 5 6   10 09 08 07 06 05

For all the writers whose stories are waiting to be told

MID-CONTINENT PUBLIC LIBRARY - BTM

3 0003 00065291 5

MID-CONTINENT PUBLIC LIBRARY
Liberty Branch
1000 Kent Street
Liberty, MO 64068

LI

Contents

Foreword

Marthe Jocelyn

Everybody has a secret.

You do, don't you?

Most people have more than one. And we usually keep the biggest secrets from those we are closest to – our families. Why do we hide things?

The stories in this book make us think about that question. Some secrets are like precious jewels held in the palm of our hand. Some secrets are lies, told to make or avoid trouble. Some secrets are scary, like a creaking door when no one is home. Some secrets cover up shame. Some secrets are special little moments you never mention to anyone. Some are part of a surprise. Others are like soda pop, waiting to burst out in a flood of giggles.

Sometimes only one person knows the secret. Often, the best part of keeping a secret is finally being able to tell someone else.

I am delighted to invite you to turn the page and share these Secrets. . . .

Father's Day

Teresa Toten

Class hadn't even started and already the chalk dust was swirling and somersaulting, trying to break out of those long skinny shards of light. It can make you mental if you try to track those things. I stood in front of the teacher's dilapidated old desk. Chalk, erasers, paper clips, and a box of HB pencils were in the first drawer on the left. A strap was all by itself in the second one, and a King James Version Bible and pink crystal rosary beads were in the bottom drawer. Each drawer on the right-hand side was locked. We all knew it.

"But see, the thing is . . . the nuns are always the worst!" I shifted from one foot to the other. "No offense, or anything."

"None taken." Sister Rose smiled. "And just why is that, Katie?"

"Well, you know, they . . . you, all make such a big deal about it, especially, especially, on the Friday before Father's Day. Everyone gets to feel all sorry for me and give me these looks of fake pity."

Sister raised one pretty eyebrow.

"And some real pity too, I suppose, but that's even worse, especially, especially, from the kids with dads but dads who aren't there, or dads who aren't even really, for sure, properly married to their moms in the first place."

This would have been enough for Mrs. Cotter, my grade five teacher back at St. David's.

"But lying is a sin, Katie."

Sister Rose was a lot tougher than she looked.

"Yeah, but, Sister, it isn't really a lie, not really. All I'm asking is that I do what I do every year, which you thought was really touching and everything when I told you about it a while ago. Remember?"

Sister nodded.

"I still make my Father's Day card, just like the rest of the class. Then, after school, I still walk over to Winston Churchill Park, which used to be our favorite, and then, then, I still bury the card in the flower bed nearest St. Clair and Spadina. And then, finally, I wish him Happy Father's Day." I gave her the smile I'd been practicing since 6:20 A.M.

Sister raised her eyebrow again.

"After I've prayed for the deliverance of his immortal soul, of course." I checked the clock – 8:25. The bell would ring at 8:30.

"So, all I'm saying, I mean asking, is that since this is a new school for me, couldn't we please, just this once, not announce to the whole class that, tragically, poor Katie O'Brian's father has passed away? And that the rest of us have to count our blessings by saying fifteen rosary rounds at recess? So, not only do they feel real sorry for me, but they hate me too because of the stupid rosary rounds. No offense. Sorry, Sister."

"None taken, Katie." She patted my hand.

Sister Rose has soft cool hands, all the time, no matter what. All nuns have soft cool hands. I don't know how they do it. It's like a holy thing.

"So, you see? We're not lying, not really, not even with that 'by omission' thing because it's not like anyone's asking. See? We just don't have to advertise it. We don't have to enter the Katie O'Brian pity party sweepstakes. Please, Sister?"

Sister Rose looked down at her hands. Her lashes seemed to shade half of her face.

"And, and . . . I've been praying on it for weeks, real hard . . . and, well, it just came to me yesterday that I bet that Jesus would be okay with this."

Sister bit her lower lip and frowned. She did this whenever she was trying to stop herself from laughing. We all knew it.

"You are impossible, Katie Magdalene O'Brian."

"That's just what my mom says, Sister."

She shook her head. I had her.

The bell rang.

"Okay, Katie," she sighed. "We won't make an announcement about your deceased father. No rosary novenas, but you'll do each and every single one at home." She put her soft cool hand on mine again. "This will be our little secret, Katie. Not a lie, just a secret."

You had to hand it to me – I was good.

We got to the card-making right after Religious Studies and French. Mary Catherine and I worked on ours together. Mary Catherine has a deeply superior creative artistic soul. Just like me. So, we've been best friends since practically my first week at St. Raymond's. Mary Catherine knows about it all, about absolutely everything. Well, except for the part where I really, really want Mr. Sutherland – that's Mary Catherine's father – to be my father.

Sometimes I want it so much, I feel like I'm vibrating.

He is such a nice dad.

Mr. Sutherland is an important businessman. He has

four different suits and a dark brown briefcase with worn handles. He works in an office with a door, in one of those big black towers on King Street. His office is on the 34th floor! One day, when school's over, Mary Catherine and me are going to meet him in his office and then we're going out for lunch.

He said.

Mr. Sutherland calls me Slugger because I'm on the Christie Pits Pirates softball team. I'm deeply artistic *and* athletic. It's a rare combination, Mr. Sutherland says. Sometimes, when he gets home early, he pours the three of us a big tall glass of Coca-Cola with lots of ice and then he asks us about school, or our friends, or just stuff. And he asks me too, not just Mary Catherine.

I hate Coca-Cola.

But, I drink it right down and I always say, "Thanks, Mr. Sutherland!" and he always winks at me and says, "Well, you're welcome, Slugger."

Mr. Sutherland is an Aqua Velva man. That's a shaving lotion. He's an Aqua Velva man because Mary Catherine first bought it for him in grade one and she hadn't turned even a little creative yet. I would buy him Old Spice because Mr. Sutherland looks just like their sailboat man in the magazines. It smells more like he should smell too. I take a whiff every single time I'm in the perfume department of Eaton's.

Anyway, Mary Catherine and I were making, hands down, the most elaborate fancy cards in the whole class. We are like that for all our projects. Father Bob says that God is in the details. Our stuff is always bursting with God. My card had an origami cross on the front and the whole thing was edged with cutout daisies. It said YOU ARE MY HERO in big 3-D letters on the front and HAPPY FATHER'S DAY TO THE BEST DAD IN THE WORLD over a pop-up striped tie on the inside.

I headed straight over to Winston Churchill right after school. Straight to the little rose garden in the corner.

I looked all sad.

You never know. Sister Rose could go right by on the streetcar, or something.

There was a newly turned spot of earth behind the orangey roses and just in front of the bushes with the green-and-yellow speckled leaves. I dug a hole with my six-inch ruler, then I folded up my card into four and buried it.

I made a sign of the cross. Not a little fast one in the middle of your chest – a big one, just in case.

I prayed.

Not for my father.

For Mary Catherine's.

I prayed that God in His infinite wisdom would figure out how to make Mr. Sutherland my father. And that He would do this without hurting Mrs. Sutherland, who is nice enough; or Mary Catherine, who is my very best friend; or my mother, who, Lord knows, has been hurt bad enough already. *Thank you very much. Amen.*

I knew it was a really tall order, but Sister always says that it is not for us to ascertain the infinite mercy that is within the mind of God. So, that means that it's up to Him to figure out the details.

I practically flew home. I felt just tons better after my little ceremony. I'd have to remember to tell Sister about that part on Monday. It was the *true* part of our little secret.

Mom and I live on top of the ALWAYS OPEN hardware, electronics, and variety store on Bathurst Street that is closed on Sundays, Mondays, and Tuesdays. We moved here last August and it's my favorite place so far. You'd never know it from the street, but most of those apartments over stores are really, really beautiful. Ours sure is. Mom and me have our own bedrooms; there's a kitchen in the back, a dinette, and a massive huge living room that looks right onto Bathurst. Our apartment is loaded with charm and personality. Mr.

Sutherland says so practically every time he drops me off from a late night at Mary Catherine's.

Mom was in the hallway before I even got my key out of the door. *Why was she home so early?*

"Katie, honey?"

I couldn't really see her in the soupy darkness of the hallway, but I could tell she was still in her white dental assistant's uniform.

"Hi, Mom, how come you're –"

"Katie? I have great news, honey."

She was using her chipped china voice. High and cracked.

There was a crash, then rattling in the kitchen. I stepped towards her, my heart racing and pounding at the same time.

"Yes, that's right, honey," she said, nodding. "Your father's home. Let's go into the living room."

Daddy?

He found us.

Mom grabbed me by the arm and mouthed, "He's a *little* drunk." The whole left side of her face was red and angry looking.

A little drunk was bad.

Very drunk was better – he'd miss you two out of three shots.

Passed out was best.

Daddy lumbered in heavily. Mom whispered, "I'm sorry, honey, I told too much," and then moved away. She said it so fast and low, I wasn't sure what I heard.

"Katie! Hey, look at you, huh!" He wasn't weaving, hardly.

Just a little drunk.

"How's my baby, huh? Give your old man a hug."

He yanked me to him. I was instantly smothered by rye and Coca-Cola. I didn't mind the reek of the Player's unfiltered cigarettes, or even his sweat. It was the dark syrupy smell of the Coke that made me gag.

Daddy rubbed my back and started to chuckle. "I'm here for the big Father's Day picnic at St. Raymond's on Sunday. Whaddya say to that, huh?"

My stomach filled up with ice cubes.

"Daddy can't wait to meet all your new friends and your new teacher. You landed a real live nun this time, eh?"

"Stephen, don't."

"Sister Rosie, or something, right?" He hugged me tighter.

"Stephen, please."

I decided not to breathe. That's how you die. From not breathing. I wondered how long it would take.

Daddy snorted and chuckled again, except it sounded more like gurgling. "S'okay, sweetcheeks. Your mom told me about your whole scam." He let go of me, thought better of it, and grabbed me by the back of my hair.

"So, I'm dead, eh?"

"Stephen!" Mom's face was beginning to swell up.

Daddy reached over to the side table and picked up his glass with his left hand, still hanging on to my hair with his right.

"You little con artist," he said, pulling my head from side to side. "You got the best of both worlds. You get a whack of sympathy from your Holy Roller nun and the rest of the class doesn't know, so if I turn up with you, no one thinks anything of it."

He took a big swig of his drink.

"Bloody brilliant." He was oozing Coca-Cola.

"You're a chip off the old block." He yanked my head back.

"*Ow*, Daddy, *ow*."

He looked down at me. "I'm proud of you, sweetie. Eleven years old and lying to a nun for God's sake, what balls!"

"No, it wasn't like . . ." My eyes welled up. "It was more like a deeply superior, creative, secret, kind of . . ."

"You mean a lie. Katie, you're mine. Don't tell me you didn't feel a thrill when she bought it."

Oh. God.

"Fruit don't fall far from the tree. You're just like me, through and through."

Like him? No. I tried to find Mom. She was way off across the living room, by the window.

Daddy turned my head back and up. He is eleven feet tall. *Like him? No.* No. It wasn't like that, not like how he said. Not exactly. I just didn't want Sister Rose to know, about . . . about him, about this. It's bad when they know. And maybe it was kind of smart to convince her to keep "our secret" from the rest of the class, just in case, but that wasn't it. Not all of it. Not really. I was hazy about how my secret lies got all started up in the first place. The details somersaulted each other, just like the classroom chalk dust. I thought, maybe, yeah, I remembered that, maybe, I sort of believed that if I told an actual real live Sister that Daddy was dead . . . that somehow . . . maybe . . . God would make it true.

Oh. God.

I was worse than him.

I'm sorry.

"You're sure not like your simpering mother. No, sir. You're all me, sweetcheeks. Daddy's little con, Daddy's little liar. Admit it, Katie."

Sorry, sorry. It was true.

No.

It *was* true. WAS. *Not after this, no sir.*

I tried to remember the Act of Contrition, but the prayer got tangled up in my head right after the *I confess to Almighty God* part. *Okay, okay.*

Our Father, who art in heaven. . . . I would march right in on Monday morning and tell Sister Rose the whole thing. *Hallowed be thy name.* Everything. *Thy kingdom come.*

Daddy didn't move.

He was waiting.

I didn't move.

I knew better.

Sister would have to tell the principal. *Thy will be done.* There'd be, like, major serious big-time penance. *Something, daily bread something.* . . . That's okay, I deserved penance; I could take it. But Sister would hate me. *And forgive us our trespasses.* . . . No, no, she wouldn't. *As we forgive those who trespass against us.* . . . Nuns take a vow about that sort of thing. *And lead us not into temptation.* It's got to do with lost sheep and Joseph and his multicolored coat, or something. *But deliver us from evil.* And then, and then, I would never lie again. *Amen.*

"Admit it, Katie."

Ever. Suddenly I was indestructible with the white hot truth of it. I was all powered on and lit up from the inside.

"Daddy's little con."

Never again.

"Admit it and I'll tell ya what, sweetie." Daddy checked his watch. "Admit it and I'm out of here. Gone. No picnic. There's an oil rig with my name on it in Alberta and my Greyhound *could* leave at 9:30. Deal?"

Never.

He let go of my hair, turned me towards him, and crouched right down. "Katie, let me know, I'm leaving a piece of me behind and I'm off. Give me that." Daddy's eyes were tearing up. He'd done that kind of thing before. A lot.

Mom started crying for real, though. Quietly. You wouldn't even know if you didn't know.

Daddy put his hands on my shoulders, really gently. "Katie girl, you're *my* little con, *my* little liar, aren't ya?"

I looked straight into his wet eyes.

Just . . . once . . . more. . . .

"Yes, Daddy," I said.

Simple Summer

Susan Adach

I loved summer because it was simple.

Not complicated like school – who to eat lunch with, does this top make me look like a dweeb, will they laugh at my crummy speech on the Loch Ness Monster? Summer was way easier. Only one bathing suit to choose, should I have my hot dog with or without ketchup, make sure you cash in enough pop bottles for change for the popcorn man *and* the Yummy Man ice-cream truck. The only rule: Be in by the time the streetlights come on. Good and simple.

That summer, it seemed like all of Thames Avenue was away. No problem, even when my dad canceled our holiday. We usually went to my Aunt Molly and Uncle George's, and their Tastee Freeze Ice Cream store in Huntsville, but my mother was having a baby soon and my dad said the long drive wasn't a good idea.

We'd have to "tough it out at home." It didn't matter. I made plans to spend the entire summer with my across-the-street best friend, Janice Muncaster. Her dad had just started a new job and they weren't going away either. *Perfect.*

The first week, just like we planned, Janice and I stretched out on two canvas cots in the shadow of the giant black walnut trees at the end of her backyard and read mystery books until our eyes were burning slits. *Heaven.*

The following Monday, Janice concentrated while putting white polish on her now tanned toes. She finished her toenails and picked up her book, but didn't open it. "Susan, you're going to hate me," she said.

Janice had just got back from the hairdresser's for her annual summer perm. Her head looked like a Kurly Kate pot scrubber. The curls coiled around like a herd of snails. Later in the summer, we were planning to put on a show in her backyard, including a musical performance – maybe something from *Annie*, so her hair was perfect. My poker-straight Buster Brown bowl cut meant I would probably be wearing a bathing cap and taking the role of the bald Daddy Warbucks.

"Hate you?" I didn't like the sound of that. "Why would I hate you?"

"We're going away. Camping."

I lost my page in *The Secret inside the Box* and sat up. "You're going away? You can't!" The words poured out of me before I could even think of swallowing them. "Where are you going? For how long? When?"

"Killarney Park, up north somewhere. For three weeks. We leave on Saturday." She winced.

"Three weeks?" *One third of the summer? I won't last. This would not, could not, happen.* "But you told me you couldn't go away because of your dad's new job." Obviously she'd forgotten this detail. Good thing I was here to remind her, so she could tell her family the camping trip was off.

Janice dug her thumb between the pages of her book. "No, we're going with my Aunt Bobbie and her two kids. Just the moms and the kids." I felt my stomach squeeze up, as if trying to hide under my ribs. "Mom says the park ranger will give us a hand if we need it. We'll have a spot on the beach. But I'll write you every day and I can get mail at the tuck shop, my mom said. I'll give you the address. And we'll each make a chart to count off the days till I'm back." My stomach popped up into my throat. She smiled like someone had just given her a needle and she was trying to put on a brave face.

I quickly looked down the driveway at the street. There were no other kids, no hide-and-seek, no Red Rover, no dogs rolling in the grass. Sure, that was because they were all somewhere right now having fun, the best times of their lives – splashing in a lake, eating Creamsicles, making crafts out of pinecones.

I looked up and saw Wayne Bleeker, three fences over, throwing a lacrosse ball in and out of his stick against the wall. A dull *whump whump* sounded each time the India rubber ball hit the concrete. Janice couldn't leave me behind with creepy people like Wayne Bleeker.

On Friday, our last day before all happiness stopped, we wore our almost-matching madras plaid shirts and shorts – mine blue, hers red. We put exactly the same things in our tote bags (comb, one Kleenex, chapstick, and two dollars), and headed up to the Met Restaurant for french fries with gravy and a Coke. Usually my favorite, the gravy congealed like a beret over my untouched fries. I dug holes into them with my fork as Janice talked about all the things they'd do camping. She couldn't help it. She'd been brainwashed, made to think this was a good idea. There's an astronomer and an anthropologist in the park, she told me, and at night they gather all the campers together to look at the stars. They also do this thing where they call the wolves, then there's a big huge bonfire and a marshmallow roast for everybody.

"We're going to look at cribs," I said, trying to keep up my end of the conversation. How could my mother have a stupid baby when I was eleven? It had ruined my entire summer!

I couldn't sleep at all that night. I watched the second hand on my alarm clock click sixty times every minute. I stopped counting at 1,027 seconds.

In the morning, from behind the veil of our living room sheers, I saw the Muncasters pack the big green station wagon. It was filled to bursting with luggage and tents and badminton rackets. Bicycles were tied to the roof rack. Mrs. Muncaster, Janice, and her sister, Lindsay, piled into the car.

I ran outside when the car's engine roared to life. "Send me a postcard!" I hollered, and waved like crazy as they pulled out of the driveway. Janice leaned out the window and pulled up her nose in a piggy salute. I did the same. The car disappeared around the corner.

"She'll be back before you know it," Mr. Muncaster called from across the street. He was cleaning his golf clubs with the garden hose. I could see he was really broken up. He didn't understand. Being without Janice was like my arm falling off.

I went into the house and crossed off the first day with black permanent marker. Then I slumped into the living room and lay on the couch, staring at the ceiling. The fan on the stereo cabinet moved back and forth, only stirring the hot air. Life as I knew it was over.

Mom came into the room, wiping her hands on a tea towel. "You've got to keep busy, Susan. Your room could use a cleanup, you know. There used to be a desk in there, but I don't think I've seen it since January. And I'm going up the street later. I could drop you off at the library and pick you up when I'm finished. Want to come?"

I couldn't move. I had no doubt that the instant boredom had paralyzed me. I continued to stare straight up.

"Suit yourself," Mom said, and went back to whatever it is moms do that keeps them busy every single minute of the day.

I felt the heat cover me like a blanket as I lay there listening to the fan whirring. Then I heard a *whump whump whump* from outside. I peeled myself off the couch and peeked out the curtain. Wayne Bleeker was bouncing his stupid lacrosse ball from his lacrosse stick on the sidewalk. I watched for a minute. I'd better go out and tell him people were trying to recuperate in here. I slipped out the screen door and onto the porch.

*

"Hi, Susan," Wayne said, without looking up at me. He kept bouncing his dumb old ball. I guessed it wouldn't hurt if I came a little closer. No need to shout. I came down the porch steps and stood on the edge of our lawn.

"Hi, Wayne." I watched him bounce the ball, pretending he didn't notice me. Janice and I pretty well ignored Wayne. She said his hair was like a tuft of wiry shoots that always looks dusty. I thought he looked like Punkin' Head in Eaton's Santa Claus Parade. He kept bouncing the ball like it was some kind of duty.

"Hey, hi." It was Franny Fenny, giggling. Franny lived at the other end of the street, but it might as well have been another city. Funny how there's a dividing line on the street. People who live beyond that border, you don't have a clue about how they live, sometimes even what their names are. But we knew Franny because all the kids were at our end, so she showed up whenever she thought there might be something going on. Franny's family was practically foreign, from Newfoundland. Her mom was loud and called people love and ducky. It seemed there was a whole brood of Fennies, either hollering or eating molasses on bread. Franny was always jumping and giggling, her dark red braids always swinging and her knees always skinned.

I never ever thought of asking her to play. She was from the other end of the street, for Pete's sake.

"What're ya doin'?" Franny asked, in a Newfoundland accent.

"Nothing." I shrugged. Wayne just kept bouncing his ball. I should go in, I thought, sit on my bed, and wait for Janice to come home. I don't want to be out here with these two.

"Want to do something?" Wayne asked. He had stopped bouncing his ball and grinned at me. His tiny pointy teeth were the color of the inside of a banana.

"Sure. What?" Franny didn't wait to see if she was included.

"Want to do something?" Wayne repeated, looking at me.

I never played with these kids. Not by myself. Only when there was a whole gang of us for British bulldog or hide-and-seek. I didn't know how to play with them by myself.

"Like what?" I asked. *Maybe? Could I . . .?*

"Want to go over to Sayvette's? Look around?" He glanced at Franny, as if this was some secret code.

She must have known the code because she immediately agreed. "Yeah, let's go to Sayvette's!" She clapped, making her braids bounce.

Sayvette's was the department store at the plaza.
The plaza was on the other side of the creek, and then
down the highway. Janice and I never went there. We
were not allowed to go there, ever.

"I haven't got any money," I said, hoping this would
be the end of it.

"Doesn't matter, we don't need money," said Wayne.
"We'll just look around. Let's go." He waited for a
moment, then turned and threw his lacrosse stick up
onto his lawn. He started walking toward the end of
Thames Avenue, which led down to the creek. Franny
skipped after him.

I looked over at the house. My mother would want
me back inside. She wouldn't want me to go with these
two. I knew it.

Franny and Wayne were at the end of the street now.
I should at least tell her, at least that. . . .

I ran after them.

At the creek we slid down the deep embankment and
ran across the rocky ground to the water's edge. The
green water twisted and swirled below. It stank like an
over-used outhouse. I could taste the smell at the back
of my throat.

Wayne led us upstream to a so-called bridge he'd

made of large rocks. As light as a squirrel on a wire, Franny hippity-hopped across to the other side. I reached out a toe and skated it across the top of the first flat rock, then pulled it back. "I can't," I said.

Wayne stood in the middle, cool as a cucumber, as if he did this one hundred times every day. He probably did. "You can do it," he said. "It's nothing."

I shook my head *no* and backed up a little.

"C'mon," he said, "give me your hand." He leaned over and threw his hand out to me, like it was a lifeline.

I backed up more and shook my head again. "No, I can't."

"C'mon, I won't let you fall. Take my hand." It was an order. What could I do?

I grabbed his hand. It was hard and dry, like the bottom of a shoe. It gripped mine as if my life depended on it. I'd never touched a boy before. It prickled up the hair on the back of my neck. He pulled me across. The whole time, once he had me, I knew I wouldn't fall.

We climbed up the hill and over the guardrail, onto the shoulder of the highway. Cars zipped past. I could hardly breathe, and it wasn't from the hot asphalt and exhaust fumes. We sang, "Dead skunk in the middle of the road, stinkin' to high heaven," at the top of our lungs. When Wayne said he was going to hang a moon

at the cars, I could feel my cheeks burning and prayed
they didn't notice. I was glad he didn't do it.

Sayvette's was busy with people on holidays looking for
air-conditioning, away from the stinky sweaty heat
outside. Moms and sticky babies, teenagers, old people.
I'd only ever come here with my mom when we had
something specific to buy. Now we were on our own
and could go wherever we wanted.

We looked at fish in tanks, bounced basketballs,
tried on sunglasses, and ate free samples of tapioca
pudding. We ended up in the candy department. I was
beginning to think this was the best time I'd ever had.
There was a table display with a kiddie wading pool on
top filled with toy boats, all different colors. It looked
pretty, like a tiny sea of rainbow baby boats. *Maybe my
baby sister* (fingers crossed) *would like one. . . .*

Wayne pressed up behind me and whispered, "Take
one."

My head came up. "What?"

"Take one," he whispered, moving past me. "Put it
in your shorts." He turned around to face me and
continued walking, backwards. "When I give the
signal, stick one of those in your shorts and run for the
exit doors."

Franny was beside me now. So close, I could feel her

breath on my shoulder. When I glanced at her, her eyes were dancing.

Wayne kept walking backwards until he stopped at the end of the display table. He whipped his head back and forth, back and forth, watching, waiting. I was shivering and gnawing my knuckle.

"Okay, now!" he hissed.

No time to think. I watched my hand reach for a red boat and stuff it down the front of my lime green shorts. I felt it scrape my belly as I shoved it past the waistband, but I didn't care. I could feel a gouge bloom on the skin of my stomach. In one motion, Wayne grabbed a large cellophane pack of twenty Doublemint gum and jammed it up under his shirt. For a crazy minute, I saw the big stupid rectangle stick out like a bulletproof vest.

"Run!" Wayne whispered fiercely.

I ran for the doors like my behind was on fire. I clamped my hands to the bottom hem of my shorts, so the little boat wouldn't drop out. I flew across the parking lot. I didn't wait to see where Franny and Wayne were. I was running blind. I ran and ran. My lungs filled up with burning hot liquid, but I kept running straight for the creek. I scrambled over the guardrail, down the hill, lost my footing and hit the ground hard.

"*Ooof.*" The air squished out of me. My knee smacked into a rock and started to throb. I didn't take the time to check for injuries, but jumped back up and limp-raced for the creek. At the water's edge, I hesitated long enough to realize if I waited one second more I'd lose my nerve. I skittered across the bridge of stones, my arms outstretched and flailing like a crazy tightrope walker. I crawled up the bank monkey-style, on all fours, my hands clawing the dirt and rock. Reaching the top, arms straight out, I surfed onto the grass and lay still.

Squealing laughter and splashing came from behind. Panting heavily, I turned over and sat up. Wayne and Franny crab-walked up the embankment. Franny flung herself onto the grass beside me and rolled back and forth, laughing herself sick. It was contagious. I could feel laughter come up from deep inside and explode out of me. I flattened myself on the grass and giggled until my stomach hurt. I put my arms around my belly and tried to stop. The sky overhead was a smooth, wonderful, Popsicle blue. Wayne's face appeared between me and the sky. His gray-green eyes crinkled up at the corners as he smiled down at me.

"You were great," he wheezed, leaning on his knees.

My laughter stopped.

"I was?" The skin on my arms goose-pimpled.

He was nodding. "Yeah, great. Fantastic." He was

doubled over, trying to catch his breath. He looked down at me and this time he winked. He held out his hand and yanked me to my feet. My whole insides quivered, like worms in a jar. He slipped the big package of gum out from under his shirt and put it into the waistband at the back of his jeans and pulled his shirt over top. I took out the toy boat, which I realized had been trapped in my underwear, and cradled it in my hand.

I could have flown home. *Nothing could be more thrilling than this.* The three of us walked along with big grins all over our faces.

Wayne turned in at his driveway. He stepped behind the hedge and reached behind his back. There was a sound of crinkling cellophane and then he held out two packages of Doublemint gum.

"Here," he said. "A reward."

Franny took hers and snickered. Mine was warm from being hidden, and I put it in my pocket. Franny didn't wait, but shoved a stick into her mouth.

"I better go," she said, through the gum. "I gotta baby-sit. Come over if ya want." This was to me, but she was almost shy about it. And then she ran off.

Wayne looked at me. "So, I'll see you tomorrow," he said. He picked up his lacrosse stick from the grass, and took his porch steps two at a time.

*

Now the sick feelings began to leak in. I tried to squash them down and make the excitement bubble up again. It almost worked.

I prayed the bulge of the boat didn't show when I told my mother I had gone to the creek with Franny Fenny and that I thought she had heard me when I called in the front door to tell her I was going. "Next time," she said, "make *sure* that I hear you." But she really seemed more interested in counting the stitches of the baby blanket she was knitting. She didn't give me the third degree like she usually did. I guess that meant *lucky me*.

I went up to my room and closed the door. The sick feelings started dribbling in again, drip by yellow drip. I lay on my bed and watched the slow-revolving ceiling fan.

This was summer. It was supposed to be simple.

It's not that Wayne and Franny were bad people. They were really fun, but the things they did . . . the things *I did*. . . .

I got up and slipped out to the backyard. I dug a hole as deep as I could and put in the toy boat. I dropped in the package of gum as well. I looked at it, sitting on the deck of the boat. I couldn't leave it there – it was a gift from Wayne. It wasn't nice to bury a gift. I snatched it up and put it back in my pocket, barely warm now.

Upstairs, I shoved the gum under my mattress, climbed into bed, and pulled the covers up tight under my chin, even though it was hot in my room.

See you tomorrow, Wayne had said. *What was I going to do about tomorrow?*

I jumped up from the bed and sat at my desk. I grabbed a piece of my best green daisy stationery and began:

Dear Janice,

Day One. Nothing much happening here. Hope you're having fun, but not too much! Seen any wolves yet? Just want to make sure we're still going to help give out the clothes baskets at the pool when you get back (and swim for free, yahoo!). Counting the days (20, in case you've lost your chart!). Write soon. Yours till the kitchen sinks.

I didn't say a word about Franny or Wayne. She wouldn't understand what had happened. Neither did I. *What would she think of me?*

I felt like that morning I had woken up as one person and now I was someone completely different. I didn't feel like the morning me anymore.

I found myself staring at the wall chart. Tomorrow, after I wrote to Janice, I was going to cross off day 20 and make it nineteen days to go. Maybe make some flowers to decorate the chart. Could take me all day tomorrow.

I got up, reached under my mattress, and removed the package of gum. It was cold now. I dropped it into my wastebasket. I crumpled up some Kleenexes and paper and dropped them on top of it.

Simple.

The Golden Darters

Elizabeth Winthrop

I was twelve years old when my father started tying flies. It was an odd hobby for a man recovering from a serious operation on his upper back, but he said at least it gave him a world over which he had some control.

The family grew used to seeing him hunched down close to his tying vise, hackle pliers in one hand, thread bobbin in the other. We began to bandy about strange phrases – foxy quills, bodkins, peacock hurl. Father's corner of the living room was off-limits to the maid because she was too careless with the vacuum cleaner. Who knew what precious bit of calf's tail or rabbit fur would be sucked away, never to be seen again?

Because of my father's illness, we had gone up to our summer cottage on the lake a month early. None of my gang of friends ever came till the end of July, so in the beginning of that summer I hung around home watching my father as he fussed with the flies. I was the only child he allowed to stand near him while he worked. "Your brothers bounce," he muttered one day. "You can stay and watch if you don't bounce."

So I took great care not to bounce, or lean, or even breathe too noisily on him while he performed his small delicate maneuvers. I had never been so close to my father for so long before. I stared at the large pores of his skin, the sleek black hair brushed straight back from his temples, the jaw muscles tightening and slackening. Something in my father seemed always to be ticking.

When he leaned over his work, his shirt collar slipped down to reveal the recent scar, a jagged trail of disrupted tissue. The tender pink skin gradually paled and then toughened during those weeks when he took his afternoon nap on our little patch of front lawn. Our house was close to the lake. It seemed to embarrass my mother to have him stretch himself out on the grass for all the swimmers and boaters to see.

"Sleep on the porch," she would say. "That's why we set the hammock up there."

"Why shouldn't a man nap on his own front lawn if

he so chooses?" he would reply. "I have to mow the bloody thing. I might as well put it to some use."

And my mother would shrug and give up.

At the table, when he was absorbed, he lost all sense of anything but the magnified insect under the light. Often when he pushed his chair back and announced the completion of his latest project, there would be a bit of down or a tuft of dubbing stuck to the edge of his lip. I did not tell him about it but stared, fascinated, wondering how long it would take to blow away. Sometimes it never did and I imagine he discovered the fluff in the bathroom mirror when he went upstairs to bed. Or maybe my mother plucked it off with one of those proprietary gestures of hers that irritated my brothers so much.

In the beginning, Father wasn't very good at the fly-tying. He was a large thick-boned man with sweeping gestures, a robust laugh, and a sudden terrifying temper. If he had not loved fishing so much, I doubt he would have persevered with the fussy business of the flies. After all, the job required tools normally associated with woman's work. Thread and bobbins, soft slippery feathers, a magnifying glass, and an instruction manual that read like a cookbook.

It said things like, "Cut off a bunch of yellowtail. Hold the tip end with the left hand and stroke out the short hairs."

But Father must have had a goal in mind. You tie flies because, one day, in the not-too-distant future, you will attach them to a tippett, wade into a stream, and lure a rainbow trout out of his quiet pool.

There was something endearing, almost childish, about his stubborn nightly ritual at the corner table. His head bent under the floor lamp, his fingers trembling slightly, he would whisper encouragement to himself, talk his way through some particularly delicate operation. Once or twice I caught my mother gazing across my brothers' heads at him. When our eyes met, she would turn away and busy herself in the kitchen.

Finally, one night, after weeks of allowing me to watch, he told me to take his seat. "Why, Father?"

"Because it's time for you to try one."

"That's all right. I like to watch."

"Nonsense, Emily. You'll do just fine."

He had stood up. The chair was waiting. Across the room, my mother put down her knitting. Even the boys, embroiled in a noisy game of double solitaire, stopped their wrangling for a moment. They were all waiting to see what I would do. My fear of failing him made me hesitate. I knew that my father put his trust in results, not in the learning process.

"Sit down, Emily."

I obeyed, my heart pounding. I was a cautious, secretive child and I could not bear to have people watch me do things. My piano lesson was the hardest hour in the week. The teacher would sit with a resigned look on her face while my fingers groped across the keys, muddling through a sonata that I had played perfectly just an hour before. The difference was that then nobody had been watching.

". . . so we'll start you off with a big hook." He had been talking for some time. *How much had I missed already?*

"Ready?" he asked.

I nodded.

"All right then, clamp this hook into the vise. You'll be making the golden darter, a streamer. A big flashy fly, the kind that imitates a small fish as it moves underwater."

Across the room my brothers had returned to their game, but their voices were subdued. I imagined they wanted to hear what was happening to me. My mother had left the room.

"Tilt the magnifying glass so you have a good view of the hook. Right. Now tie it on with the bobbin thread."

It took me three tries to line the thread up properly on the hook, each silken line nesting next to its neighbor. "We're going to do it right, Emily, no matter how long it takes."

"It's hard," I said quietly.

Slowly I grew used to the tiny tools, to the oddly enlarged view of my fingers through the magnifying glass. They looked as if they didn't belong to me anymore. The feeling in their tips was too small for their large clumsy movements. Despite my father's repeated warnings, I nicked the floss once against the barbed hook. Luckily it did not give way.

"It's Emily's bedtime," my mother called from the kitchen.

"Hush, she's tying in the throat. Don't bother us now."

I could feel his breath on my neck. The mallard barbules were stubborn, curling into the hook in the wrong direction. Behind me, I sensed my father's fingers twisting in imitation of my own.

"You've almost got it," he whispered, his lips barely moving. "That's right. Keep the thread slack until you're all the way around."

I must have tightened it too quickly. I lost control of the feathers in my left hand, the clumsier one. First the gold Mylar came unwound and then the yellow floss.

"Damn it all, now look what you've done!" he roared, and, for a second, I wondered whether he was talking to me. He sounded as if he were talking to a grown-up. He sounded the way he had just the night before when an antique teacup had slipped through my mother's soapy fingers and shattered against the hard surface of the sink. I sat back slowly, resting my aching spine against the chair for the first time since we'd begun.

"Leave it for now, Gerald," my mother said tentatively from the kitchen. Out of the corner of my eye, I could see her sponging the counter with small defiant sweeps of her hand. "She can try again tomorrow."

"What happened?" called a brother. They both started across the room towards us, but stopped at a look from my father.

"We'll start again," he said, his voice once more under control. "Best way to learn. Get back on the horse."

With a flick of his hand, he loosened the vise, removed my hook, and threw it into the wastepaper basket.

"From the beginning?" I whispered.

"Of course," he replied. "There's no way to rescue a mess like that."

My mess had taken almost an hour to create.

"Gerald," my mother said again. "Don't you think –"

"How can we possibly work with all these interruptions?" he thundered. I flinched as if he had hit me. "Go on upstairs, all of you. Emily and I will be up when we're done. Go on, for God's sake. Stop staring at us."

At a signal from my mother, the boys backed slowly away and crept up to their room. She followed them. I felt all alone, as trapped under my father's piercing gaze as the hook in the grip of its vise.

We started again. This time my fingers were trembling so much that I ruined three badger hackle feathers, stripping off the useless webbing at the tip. My father did not lose his temper again. His voice dropped to an even, controlled monotone that scared me more than his shouting.

After an hour of painstaking labor, we reached the same point with the stubborn mallard feathers curling into the hook. Once, twice, I repinched them under the throat, but each time they slipped away from me. Without a word, my father stood up and leaned over me. With his cheek pressed against my hair, he reached both hands around and took my fingers in his. I longed to surrender the tools to him and slide away off the chair, but we were so close to the end. He captured the curling stem with the thread and trapped it in place with three quick wraps.

"Take your hands away carefully," he said. "I'll do the whip finish. We don't want to risk losing it now."

I did as I was told, sat motionless with his arms around me, my head tilted slightly to the side so he could have the clear view through the magnifying glass. He cemented the head, wiped the excess glue from the eye with a waste feather, and hung my golden darter on the tackle box handle to dry. When at last he pulled away, I breathlessly slid my body back against the chair. I was still conscious of the havoc my clumsy hands or an unexpected sneeze could wreak on the table, which was cluttered with feathers and bits of fur.

"Now, that's the fly you tied, Emily. Isn't it beautiful?"

I nodded. "Yes, Father."

"Tomorrow, we'll do another one. An olive grouse. Smaller hook, but much less complicated body. Look. I'll show you in the book."

As I waited to be released from the chair, I didn't think he meant it. He was just trying to apologize for having lost his temper, I told myself, just trying to pretend that our time together had been wonderful.

But the next morning, when I came down late for breakfast, he was waiting for me with the materials for the olive grouse already assembled. He was ready to start in again, to take charge of my clumsy fingers with his voice and talk them through the steps.

That first time was the worst, but I never felt comfortable at the fly-tying table with Father's breath tickling the hair on my neck. I completed the olive grouse, another golden darter to match the first, two muddler minnows, and some others. I don't remember all the names anymore.

Once I hid upstairs, pretending to be immersed in my summer-reading books, but he came looking for me.

"Emily," he called. "Come on down. Today we'll start the leadwinged coachman. I've got everything set up for you."

I lay very still and did not answer.

"Gerald," I heard my mother say. "Leave the child alone. You're driving her crazy with those flies."

"Nonsense," he said, and started up the dark wooden stairs, one heavy step at a time.

I put my book down and rolled slowly off the bed, so that by the time he reached the door of my room I was on my feet, ready to be led back downstairs to the table.

Although we never spoke about it, my mother became oddly insistent that I join her on trips to the library or the general store.

"Are you going out again, Emily?" my father would

call after me. "I was hoping we'd get some work done on this minnow."

"I'll be back soon, Father," I'd say. "I promise."

"Be sure you are," he said.

Then, at the end of July, my old crowd of friends from across the lake began to gather and I slipped away to join them early in the morning, before my father got up.

The girls were a gang. When we were all younger, we'd held bicycle relay races on the ring road and played down at the lakeside together under the watchful eyes of our mothers. Every July, we threw ourselves joyfully back into each other's lives. That summer we talked about boys and smoked illicit cigarettes in Randy Kidd's basement, and held leg-shaving parties in her bedroom behind a safely locked door. Randy was the ringleader. She was the one who suggested we pierce our ears.

"My parents would die," I said. "They told me I'm not allowed to pierce my ears until I'm seventeen."

"Your hair's so long, they won't even notice," Randy said. "My sister will do it for us. She pierces all her friends' ears at college."

In the end, only one girl pulled out. The rest of us sat in a row, with the obligatory ice cubes held to our ears, waiting for the painful stab of the sterilized needle.

Randy was right. At first my parents didn't notice. Even when my ears became infected, I didn't tell them. All alone in my room, I went through the painful procedure of twisting the gold studs and swabbing the recent wounds with alcohol. Then, on the night of the club dance, when I had changed my clothes three times and played with my hair in front of the mirror for hours, I came across the small plastic box with dividers in my top bureau drawer. My father had given it to me so that I could keep my flies in separate compartments, untangled from one another. I poked my finger in and slid one of the golden darters up along its plastic wall. When I held it up, the Mylar thread sparkled in the light, like a jewel. I took out the other darter, hammered down the barbs of the two hooks, and slipped them into the raw holes in my earlobes.

Someone's mother drove us all to the dance and Randy and I pushed through the side door into the ladies' room. I put my hair up in a ponytail, so the feathered flies could twist and dangle above my shoulders. I liked the way they made me look – free and different and dangerous, even. And they made Randy notice.

"I've never seen earrings like that," she said. "Where did you get them?"

"I made them with my father. They're flies. You know, for fishing."

"They're great! Can you make me some?"

I hesitated. "I have some others at home I can give you," I said at last. "They're in a box in my bureau."

"Can you give them to me tomorrow?" she asked.

"Sure," I said, with a smile. Randy had never noticed anything I'd worn before. I went out to the dance floor, swinging my ponytail in time to the music.

My mother noticed the earrings as soon as I got home.

"What has gotten into you, Emily? You know you were forbidden to pierce your ears until you were in college. This is appalling."

I didn't answer. My father was sitting in his chair behind the fly-tying table. His back was better by that time, but he still spent most of his waking hours in that chair. It was as if he didn't like to be too far away from his flies, as if something might blow away if he weren't keeping watch.

I saw him look up when my mother started in on me. His hands drifted ever so slowly down to the surface of the table as I came across the room towards him. I leaned over so that he could see my earrings better in the light.

"Everybody loved them, Father. Randy says she wants a pair too. I'm going to give her the muddler minnows."

"I can't believe you did this, Emily," my mother said, in a loud nervous voice. "It makes you look so cheap."

"They don't make me look cheap, do they, Father?" I swung my head so he could see how they bounced and my hip accidentally brushed the table. A bit of rabbit fur floated up from its pile and hung in the air for a moment before it settled back down on top of the foxy quills.

"For God's sake, Gerald, speak to her," my mother said, from her corner.

He stared at me for a long moment as if he didn't know who I was anymore, as if I were a trusted associate who had committed some treacherous and unspeakable act. "That is not the purpose for which the flies were intended," he said.

"Oh, I know that," I said quickly. "But they look good this way, don't they?"

He stood up and, across the top of the table lamp, considered me in silence for a long time.

"No, they don't," he finally said. "They're hanging upside down."

Then he turned off the light and I couldn't see his face anymore.

I Don't Have to Tell You Everything

Loris Lesynski

What was it the school secretary was saying? I wondered. Fudgey or Fi-ji? No, it was 5-G. That's where I was being dumped. This was back in April, when my mom and I had just moved here. Or, run away from home was more the way I saw it.

All the other grade fives were full. The secretary triple-checked my name, Ruthie Naimie, as people always do. The computer entered it into the 5-G class list and that was that.

I soon found out that the 5-G room is in the furthest corner of this crumbling, ancient school. Dozens of cardboard boxes and eleven broken desks are jammed together at the back, with the seventeen students at the front.

The 5-G class turned out to be a real mishmash. Some of the kids are school-haters, who jeer loudly or doze off, like Steven – "Stooge" – who has done grade five at least once before. I bet he's close to thirteen. Then there's a handful of techno-geniuses, who must have got lost on the way to the gifted class. (Do gifted kids get lost?) And eccentrics like Eustace, who looks like a second-grader and has all kinds of gear hanging from his belt. The two girls at the back spend all day trying on lip gloss and eyeliner, and the ESL kids only talk to each other, which is weird because all their first languages are different.

Like I said, a real mishmash. Maybe 5-G took in all the leftovers. There was no one I could imagine being friends with. Luckily I wasn't interested in new friends.

The one good part about not making new friends is not having to talk about any of the personal stuff going on in my life. And luckily Miss Goatherd isn't like some teachers who make you write a journal as part of your schoolwork and then read it aloud. This is sure fine with me.

Sometimes I'd find myself trying to join girls in another class. Until the time one of them pointed at me and loudly informed the others that I was a 5-G-er, "You know, the garbage class." I stopped fast. *Garbage class?* How totally insulting. And that girl thought I was like them! I marched away. Who'd want to be friends with someone like her, anyway?

But then I overheard it again. Was 5-G called that by all the kids? What did they consider garbagey? The guys like Stooge who were repeating? The kids from other countries? The room we're in? None of those were good reasons. But what if that label stuck to me?

I wanted people to point at me for good reasons.

The main thing – okay, maybe the only thing – that I have going for me is being able to draw. At my old school, I was best known for a mural I painted on the wall of the stairwell. I thought maybe I could try that here.

But not on a wall. Because, on my first day here, I told my mom, "The place is falling apart! They should tear it down!" Then, on my second day, they announced that they were demolishing the entire school as soon as term was over. They've already started hammering and bashing at the portables in the playground. Not because of me, just a coincidence.

The demolition art project, though, that was because of me. This is how it happened.

The wreckers started putting wooden hoardings around the school to keep people away from the rubble. To anyone else, hoardings look like big plain sheets of plywood. But, as soon as I saw them, I thought, hey, that's where I could paint. Something fabulous and noticeable, one or two panels at the entrance to the school. In extra-high-gloss paint.

I suggested to Miss Goatherd that the school's neighbors would rather look at art than at plain plywood. I could imagine my finished panels photographed for the local newspaper. After the demolition was over, they'd pry them off the fence, frame them, and keep them at the Board of Education office. I bet they'd offer me some kind of prize.

"Wonderful!" said Miss Goatherd. "We'll have a grade five mural project!"

Rats.

She blathered on. It could come under the Peer Partner Cooperation Whatsit Something Program, she said.

That was yesterday. Today we're supposed to start. Each team will paint one panel, about the size of two regular doors side by side. We have the whole twelve days till school's out. I guess Miss Goatherd is as sick of reviews as we are.

My partners are Androullah Mortzopoulos and Lizzie Nelson. I do not want partners. I want to paint alone. I don't want to get all chummy and close with girls I hardly know. Not now.

The morning bell clangs hysterically, like it's taking its last breath. Miss Goatherd is rummaging in the cupboard. Kids are jamming themselves through the door of 5-G, just what I'm at my desk early to avoid. I keep a lookout for Androullah coming in. There she is. Androullah has so much hair, it fills the doorway of 5-G, like hundreds of curly black telephone cords sticking out every which way.

"Heyyyy!!!" comes an angry shout from behind her. Ah, partner number two – that small but mean girl, Lizzie. "Move, you!"

Androullah jolts forward and the telephone cords wave around like tentacles. Lizzie never gets caught. Only a teacher hanging from the ceiling could actually see it happen. Androullah doesn't get mad, though. She only started here two weeks ago. Why would someone come to a new school for the last month of classes? I bet she's been in some kind of trouble. Looking at her, I'm guessing it was interesting, cool trouble.

She makes a melodramatic sweeping do-come-in motion, as if she's Lizzie's doorman. *Ha!* laugh the kids who see it. They're right on the verge of a yell-fest when Miss Goatherd backs out of the supply cupboard. A boxful of pink erasers falls out with her and they *boiiiing* all over the floor. The room shakes with the noise of jackhammering outside, and a few flakes of plaster float down from the ceiling. Fake snow in this June heat wave.

"Settle down, people," says Miss Goatherd several times, tapping the tips of her fingers together. As a noiseless clap, it's so effective the yelling drops one percent.

"Morning, Miss Gauthière," singsongs Androullah, pronouncing it extracorrectly. She doesn't care about the snickers. Androullah glides over the kids picking up erasers and floats down to her desk as smoothly as someone on TV. Her T-shirt today, big enough for three scrawny Lizzies, is bright purple. Her canvas backpack has black Magic Marker drawings on it, ones she's done herself. In my old life, I might have tried being friends with someone like her. Not now, though. Androullah is very bouncy. Exactly the kind of person who's bound to ask personal questions when you least expect it.

Miss Goatherd does one last morning of math review. One thing I like about her class is being allowed to doodle all the time. Miss Goatherd's theory is that you can actually learn more from a lecture on desert plant life, fractions, or even French verbs, when you're doodling and your Right Brain is busy. Or Left Brain. I can never get them straight. Which might say something about my own brain that I don't want to know.

I turn sideways to watch Lizzie and Androullah, first one way and then the other. I bet they make the sides of these plastic seats sharp on purpose. They order the factory to manufacture seats guaranteed to keep every grade-five behind facing front. If behinds can face front. I laugh inside at my own joke and ignore where the seat is making permanent dents in me.

Lizzie isn't doodling. She's covering each page of a large notebook from top to bottom in solid black. When I first got here in April, she was about three-quarters of the way through the notebook. Now she's almost at the end. Lizzie's constant bad temper makes me very nervous. I have enough of that at home.

Androullah is drawing, not doodling.

Just before the recess bell, the PA system comes on, crackling and hissing. I'm being called to the office.

I rush down the hall. My mom's on the phone, something about the counseling session with my dad getting moved so she'll be late picking me up. We're supposed to go buy stuff for our crummy, tiny, ugly apartment. I hate this, wondering if we're ever going back home. Wondering if we do, will the arguing go on? Why did it start in the first place? Tears press sharply against my eyes.

Back when we left, I asked my mom why. "It wasn't that bad," I said.

She told me she'd hidden the really bad parts from me on purpose. I couldn't believe they were fighting even more than I knew. It made me furious in two ways:

first of all that they did it, and second that they kept it a secret.

"Why didn't you tell me?" I shouted.

Her answer was firm and matter-of-fact. "I don't have to tell you everything."

Now, I try to keep my mom on the phone, but she's been able to hear both bells – the one at the start of recess and the one at the end. She tells me to get back to the classroom.

I wish I could say that to people, *I don't have to tell you everything*. I feel obligated to answer questions. I don't know why. If I could sound as cool and confident as someone like Androullah, no one would be nosy with me. Even if I said it prickly and bad-tempered like Lizzie, it would be better than babbling on. I'd like to be the kind of person who doesn't babble on.

But I'm not. In May, after I'd been here about a month and didn't speak much to anybody, I was in the school library one afternoon. My mom and dad were crowding my brain and I was feeling pretty blue, so I hid out in TEEN FICTION H-M. This girl, Kathryn, from 5-A headed over and said hey, hi, are you okay, you're new here, right? I thought I could answer casually, but my voice came out way too high and gaspy. It was like the top coming off a warm bottle of pop that's been rolling around in the car. Suddenly I was fizzing on about how I couldn't get used to it here, how my other school was great, how really happy I was there, except that my parents think arguing is an Olympic event they have to constantly train for. My eyes started dripping. I took a breath, but continued even faster: how it got really bad and then worse, how my mom and I moved to this apartment on Wendell – it's horrible and I don't know what's going to happen. Then I said sorry, sorry for crying. And somewhere in there I think I told her my name, wrong, and finally, finally, I sputtered to a stop.

All this talking had backed up inside of me. Rule out secret agent as possible career choice. If a stranger had done that to me, bawling away in the back of the library, I'd feel like a dope trying to think what to say.

Kathryn, however, stared at me with her eyes wide-open and completely still. She didn't blink. Probably didn't breathe. In spite of the fizzing, I thought this was a very cool way to avoid saying anything and made a mental note to try it out sometime. I couldn't tell if she was friendly or making fun of me. I knew she looked disgusted when I told about my parents fighting. Good thing I didn't mention the time my mom threw the mayonnaise. Or other things. Stuff that might be funny in a puppet show or a cartoon, but not in real life. Not in my life. Stuff I don't want people to know. Since then I try to imagine that my lips are KrazyGlued together, so I don't blurt out my life story again.

When I get back to the class after talking to my mom, Miss Goatherd is just finishing her instructions for the mural project. 5-G astonishes me by being mildly enthusiastic. We line up in our teams and head for the gym.

A packet of huge sheets of newsprint has just arrived, donated by the local newspaper. Miss Goatherd instructs us to do lots of individual rough sketches first, then work out our ideas together. After that we'll move outdoors, put a coat of white primer on the plywood, and paint!

While Lizzie sullenly goes to get pencils and erasers, I tell Androullah, "This whole mural thing, it was my idea, you know."

"Wow, really?" she says, impressed. And she describes the idea she's come up with: Violetville, with a pale lilac sky. It sounds pretty good. I imagine all the people wearing striped and dotted purple outfits.

Then Androullah speaks to me in a low voice, "Hey, you want a good art tip?"

I shrug. "Sure."

"Don't ever empty a can of paint into your teacher's purse."

"What?"

"*Unless,*" she says, dragging it out, "you want to get kicked out of school and sent off to live with your aunt, someplace where you don't know *any*body. But maybe then your teacher would stop dating your dad, don't you think?"

Wow. I have no idea how to answer. I stare at Androullah with my eyes completely still and wide-open, not blinking. Excellent time for Lizzie to return with our supplies.

It feels wonderful to make huge sweeping pencil strokes on big paper and to work on the floor after months squinched up at a desk. Working alone, that's the best. I wish it could stay like this. The rest of the room bustles with talking and the crackle of the big sheets of paper. At lunchtime, everybody eats with one hand and keeps drawing with the other. My partners are on either side, but we're not talking. We're not being shy, it's more like we're way down inside ourselves.

In the afternoon, Miss Goatherd sends the class outside for a break. The three of us start to go in different directions, but she calls out, "Stay in your groups, people. Discuss what you're doing."

A couple of the rougher 5-G boys and the two makeup girls push past us, horsing around, hooting and shoving.

"*Ow!*" I make a face as they strut away. "I do not belong in this class!" I say it low and grumbly, but it must have come out sounding stuck-up because Lizzie glares at me and snaps, "Like I do?"

Maybe she's bugged by the garbage class label too. Hey, maybe even tattooed, grade-repeating Stooge doesn't appreciate it.

"It wuzza mistake, Warden," says Androullah, in a movie-gangster voice, "I was framed, framed, I tell ya."

We sit on the grass at the edge of the playground to wait out the break time. Lizzie is picking at the dry grass and whining about the heat. I'm so tense I might as well be sitting on broken glass. That's how Lizzie looks, too.

Androullah suddenly says, very seriously, "Okay, you guys, you probably wonder why I'm here." She pauses until we both look right at her. "I mean, at the school, so late in the year and everything."

Ack. I shrink inside. If she tells her stuff, maybe I'll have to tell mine. I don't want to. Once I start, who knows how much will come out of my mouth? Also, I don't want to know what trouble Androullah got into before coming here (let's face it, I have a clue). I don't really want to know about Lizzie either, what makes her so angry. Probably it's something horrible at home. And double probably, she'd clobber me five seconds after spilling.

All I have to say to Lizzie is, there are other colors besides black. All I want to talk to Androullah about is drawing.

But Androullah fools us.

"I suppose," she proclaims dramatically, "that I can at last reveal this to you both, but it's *top secret*. We're displaced Grecian royalty, my family, the Mortzopouloses, and we must roam from town to town. I'm actually the famous Princessa Androullianna. But I must learn to behave exactly like the commoners. Will you teach me, my loyal subjects? In exchange, I shall let you be royalty too and we will practice our royal deportment together."

She's so gushy and silly, Lizzie and I snort in disbelief. There's a peculiar noise coming out of Lizzie. I think it's giggling.

"My turn, now!" she says. "Okay, um . . . all right. . . . Okay, absolute top secret for me, too. I suppose you've heard of the Witness Protection Program? Well, it really works, man. I'm this awesome criminal mastermind, but I'm hiding out with a fake family and going to this rat hole school because nobody would think to look for me here. You gotta admit, this is a brilliant disguise."

"I don't know," says Androullah. "I'm pretty sure Stooge is an FBI informant. What did you witness? Or do? Jewel-thieving? Embezzlement? At the very least, can you reveal to us your real name?"

"Clandestina Von Trillium-Marmalade," says Lizzie, "but of course, if you tell, I'll have to have you killed." I didn't know Lizzie could be funny.

"Right," says Androullah, "by Eustace. He's got the lethal miniflashlight." And she pretends to whack Lizzie to death using an abandoned Popsicle stick.

Then she turns to me. "Now, Ruthie Naimie, if that is your real namie, tell us the truth and nothing but the truth." She slips off her sandal to use as a microphone.

Hey, I say to my brain, *remember when you used to know how to play along?*

"It's my parents," I say woefully. "My parents WILL NOT STOP fighting." I look shiftily from left to right. "It's ever since we won the fifty million dollars." I do a fake sob with my voice. "In order to claim it, we must agree on how to spend it. My dad wants to buy a castle in the Swiss Alps and my mom wants –" I pause "– a giant beach house mansion on the ocean, in the middle of the movie stars."

"What do you want?" asks Lizzie.

"I don't care," I say, "as long as half the money gets used to hire lots and lots of servants. Then nobody would ever get mad because the housework, or lawn mowing, or whatever, would always be done." Boy, that really *would* help.

"So," I continue, "I'm temporarily in 5-G to escape the hordes of gold diggers who want to marry me. And, of course, you are both totally invited to come spend the summer at whichever place we decide on."

Miss Goatherd is calling us back in.

Everybody loves it when it's time for the painting to begin, even the kids who can't hold a brush properly. Androullah and I go around showing them how. Some kids are doing just stripes or spirals. Three teams from 5-G and four from another class combined their panels to do an ocean scene. So far, our own panel, Purpleland – we changed the name – is gorgeous.

For Lizzie, Androullah, and me, it's as if we've made a pact without spelling it out in a lot of words. We're just not going to ask each other certain questions. Yet, anyway. And maybe creative lying, or exaggerating, or just goofing around with a tall story, any of that's okay. This makes me feel a lot safer. Clamming up is only a medium-good way to sidestep personal questions. It gets kind of lonely.

The three of us talk our heads off. Laughing, joking, and painting, a pretty good combination. I'm not that interested anymore in whether I get known for the best painting.

I think about asking Androullah why, really, she came here. But I don't.

I start to ask Lizzie about what makes her do the black notebook pages. But I stop.

I don't need to know.

The Gift

Julie Johnston

"And if I let you go," Rosalind's mother said, "you are not to set foot inside that house." She meant the house where the old women lived. They were aunts of her mother and Aunt Lydia.

Ros had a hazy memory of them – one thin, one fat. "She'll have to be told sometime," she thinks one of them said. She'd been almost too small to remember, except that she does.

"I won't go in their house," Ros said. "Anyway, it's miles from the farm. Why would I?"

And so her mother agreed to let her visit her cousin Cornelius in the country for the Christmas holidays. "And I want you to eat every scrap on your plate. There's a Depression on, young lady. I won't have you wasting food at Aunt Lydia's."

Rosalind nodded. *As long as it's not turnips.*

*

And here she was, on the train, alone. The trip took an hour, giving her time to think. Holidays were the only good things about school. No Gertie Goss for over a week. Gertie Goss, her archenemy, called her stuck-up and said stupid things, like "You've got a crazy sister!"

"Have not!" Ros called back. "You have!"

"Have so! You can ask my mother!"

Ros had five sisters and not one was the least bit crazy. Beatrice, the oldest, was too pretty for her own good, their mother said, but that didn't make her crazy. Marietta was brainy and was studying to be a doctor. Vanessa was grouchy and nearly finished high school. And Sylvia and Cynthia, the twins, were ... well, twins. There wasn't much else you could say about them, except that they weren't crazy, either.

She would be happy to see her cousin Corny. He was bossy, but so was she. They made a good pair when they got together, usually in summer at her place. He taught her to play gin rummy and she taught him to climb trees, even though he was afraid of heights. "Look up to where you're going, not down to where you've been," she told him. And, sweating, puffing, he would inch upward, his eyes on hers, mesmerized. They were both eleven.

The train slowed, whistle hallooing, bell clanging,

steam billowing past her window. She had her coat on before the conductor told her this was her stop.

On her second afternoon at the farm, the doorbell rang.

"Now who in the world . . .?" Aunt Lydia got to the door before Corny and Ros. She had her sewing circle ladies in the parlor. No one else was expected. The village doctor stood in the open porch, bending away from the wind, clamping his hat to his head. His car idled in the laneway.

"Your aunt Nell's in bad shape, Lydia," he said, stepping inside and removing his hat. "Took a weak turn in the night. They got a neighbor to call me and I was out to see her early this morning." He shook his head. "She's not good."

He and Aunt Lydia exchanged a knowing glance. "I thought, when you go out, you could take her something for pain." He handed Lydia a brown bottle with a prescription label on it.

"Oh, dear, I've got the ladies here and John's away."

The doctor looked at Corny. "The lad could take it, if he bundles up. I'd go again myself, but I've an office full of patients."

Corny stepped forward, his chest rising. The doctor looked him squarely in the eye. "And don't do anything to rile poor Lucy. She knows something's up."

"He won't," Lydia called after him. "He's good with her." She closed the door.

"May I go, too?" Ros asked. She felt redness creep up the sides of her neck, remembering her promise. She could hear the ladies in the parlor, someone talking, a little burst of laughter.

Aunt Lydia was preoccupied. "I'll make up a basket," she said. "Christmas cake and some beef tea."

"May I?"

"I think not." She frowned as if she, too, remembered something.

"But there's nothing else to do." Rosalind followed her into the kitchen, where her aunt hurriedly lined a four-quart basket with a tea towel. Corny was putting his coat on. More laughter from the parlor.

"Please?" She had a way of pleading with her dark eyes that was irresistible.

Her aunt looked at her and sighed. "Oh, I guess so. You can wait outside while Cornelius takes the basket in. You're to come straight back, both of you. You're not to stay, son, with your great-aunt Nell so sick." She handed him the basket.

Excited, Rosalind quickly thrust her arms into her coat and pulled her tam on over her fair hair, down over her ears. Something was going to happen. She didn't know why, she didn't know what, but it gave her a rushing feeling in her chest.

"Wait up!" she called to Corny, as the door slammed behind her. She wasn't doing anything wrong. Her mother had forbidden her to go into the house, and so she wouldn't.

"Let's take a shortcut," she said, when she'd caught up to Corny.

"How do you know the shortcut?" The earflaps on his hat were tied under his chin, giving him a half-strangled look.

Ros shrugged. "Just a guess." She led him up a snowy lane, into a grove of trees.

"You've never even visited them before," he said.

"I know. Here, I'll carry the basket for a while."

Soon there were tree trunks on all sides, their bare branches groaning in the wind. "I'd better lead the way," Corny said. "You'll get us lost."

She followed for a while, lugging the basket, impatient. She thought that if they veered to the left, they'd get there faster. She got ahead of him, but he skirted her, wanting to be the leader. They jockeyed for position. She pushed him aside and, without meaning to, knocked him face first into a low-hanging bough.

"Sorry," she said.

"Now look what you did!" Blood ran from his nose over his upper lip, and he spat it out.

"Hold snow up to it." She felt badly.

Their progress was slowed by Corny scooping up snow every few minutes, only to throw it down when it got too cold on his nose. Behind them gleamed a red-spotted trail of frozen clots.

They were protected from the wind by the dense bush, but the cold bit through Ros's mitts. At last they reached a clearing and saw, ahead of them, the shore of a frozen lake. On the far side huddled a log house, smoke painted in the air above its chimney.

"That's it, isn't it?" she said.

"Maybe." Corny looked sideways at her. "How come you know so much?"

She shrugged, surprised herself. "Just guessing."

The ice beckoned, blue-black where the wind had swept it bare of snow. They bounded to the edge to test its strength.

"You go first," Corny said.

"It'll be all right. Don't worry." At the very edge, the ice was lacy with cracks. Ros stepped out and the ice held. She dug with her heel, and it held. She jumped on it. A resounding crack boomed across the entire lake, sending little shock waves of sound, causing a rumble in the lake's watery underbelly. They both screamed, but the ice held.

"Go out a little farther," Corny said.

Oh, sure. "If I go through, you have to save me."

"I will."

She wouldn't go through. Still, she imagined the scene, her arms flailing in icy water, Corny running back and forth onshore, barking ideas: *Grab hold of something. Keep your head up.* She smiled, testing herself against the ice's hidden power.

By the time she was halfway across, Corny joined her. They ran over hillocks of snow and slid on the windswept patches of ice, pausing to exclaim at a leaf frozen in midswirl, and a frog, embedded, limbs outstretched in immortal breaststroke. The lake groaned in vain. They skipped ashore on the other side and heard its empty gulp.

"I hope we don't run into Lucy," Corny said.

"Who's Lucy?"

"She lives with the old aunts, but we're not supposed to talk about her in public. She's batty."

"I'm not public," she said. "What does she look like?"

"The hind end of a pig."

"What's so batty about her?"

"She rocks back and forth like a rocking horse, and she keeps patting her mouth as if she can't remember what she was going to say."

"Is she old?"

"Don't know. Looks old, but I think she's young. Mother says she's smart and dumb at the same time. Born that way. The aunts take care of her because they never want her put in an asylum, or any place like that."

They legged it over the snowbank bordering the road and up the lane to the side of the house, keeping an eye out for Lucy. In spite of the cold, Rosalind felt sweat on her upper lip. "I'll wait out here for you," she said.

Corny took the basket and vanished into a dark shed-like entry. She waited, stamping her freezing feet. A sound drew her to a wall of firewood stacked to the left of the entry. *Nothing.* She put her hands in her pockets. Again, the whispery sound. A mouse, she decided.

"*Ssss,*" it said.

She wanted to believe it was a mouse, even a snake, cold as it was. But her heart, thumping, told her it was human.

"*Ssss.*"

Her skin tingled as if she were about to touch a hot burner. She whirled suddenly. Behind her stood a slack-lipped woman in a ragged fur coat. She clutched a stick of wood as though it were a baseball bat aimed at

Rosalind's head. Ros stopped breathing, her legs soupy.

"Now, that'll do, Lucy!" A stump of an old woman appeared from the darkness of the doorway. "She won't hurt you, young lady. She likes to tease. Lucy, you get in here right this minute. You, come in too, out of the cold. Sure it's not a day to be out."

Lucy scuttled sideways into the house, shielding her backside from the old woman whose hand was raised in a threat. Helpless with fear, Rosalind allowed herself to be yanked in after her.

The large kitchen was warm and pungent with wood-smoke and spices. Ros took her eyes off the old woman long enough to notice a narrow staircase running up one wall of the room. Lucy was nowhere in sight. Corny sat at a table, a plate in front of him, his mouth crammed full of gingery-smelling cake. The woman sat Rosalind down across from Corny. He shrugged helplessly.

Ros watched the old hag bustle about the stove, creaking its door open, bending to look in. Ros wrapped her arms around herself, aware of how skinny she was beneath her coat. Had the old woman been sizing her up? Had she stumbled into some kind of fairy tale?

"Need some meat on those bones, missy," the woman said. She shoved more wood in the stove. A big pot of water steamed on top. She busied herself over the basket they'd brought, taking out each item, squinting at it with one eye.

"What's this? Medicine, is it?"

"The doctor sent it," Corny said.

She sat down on the chair next to Rosalind and offered the plate of gingerbread. "No, thanks," Ros murmured, leaning as far away from her as possible. She shouldn't have come. She should get up and leave.

The old woman grinned, exposing a perfect row of teeth, lowers only. "Want some coffee?"

"*Mmp!*" Ros's lips were pressed tight. She pushed her fair hair out of her eyes and back under her tam. Except for the pounding of her heart, they sat in silence while Corny wedged more cake into his face. She felt trapped in some other world.

The woman reached for a pair of wire-rimmed spectacles on a shelf beside the stove and put them on. She inspected Rosalind.

"So. The young lad tells me you belong to my niece Adele, her youngest. I'm your great-aunt Eileen. Your sisters are well?" The words sounded chewed. Rosalind nodded. "All still at home?"

"Yes," Rosalind managed, forgetting about Marietta at university.

"Your mother had six sisters, too, did you know that? And her the youngest."

"I only have five," said Ros.

Eileen wheezed out a laugh. "We were there at your christening, Nell and me. Up and about then, Nell was. You were done late, a toddler. How old are you, now?"

"Eleven."

"Time you were told," she said. "May never come a better chance with Nell in the state she's in, and Lord only knows how long she'll last." She pocketed the bottle of medicine. "Come along then, girl."

With both hands on Rosalind's shoulders, she pitched her out of the chair, forcing her to her feet.

White with fear, Rosalind tried to clutch at Corny, but he shrank away. "Just go," he said. "They won't hurt you if you act polite."

Still grasping her shoulders Eileen tried to escort Ros from the kitchen, but she balked, wriggling to get free.

"*Ssss!*" she heard then. Upstairs, leaning over the banister, Lucy's pug-nosed face threatened from under her heavy brow. She made a move to come down the stairs.

Ros needed no further encouragement. She went with Eileen through the dimly lit passage and into a parlor reeking of coal oil and mothballs. Great-Aunt Nell's bedroom was behind the parlor.

A square bed was anchored at the corners by spooled posts. On the bedside table, propped against a Bible, an orange jaw of false uppers grinned malignantly – the other half of Eileen's teeth. In the bed lay a tissue-paper skeleton.

"She doesn't look it, but she's awake," Eileen said. "Nell!" she shouted, "Adele's girl is here. The youngest."

The old woman opened one rheumy eye and then the other. Rosalind tried to back away.

"She won't bite you." Eileen's nudging fingers urged her closer.

"Are you the one, then?" Nell whispered. "Eileen, fetch me the spectacles." Eileen took them off her own face and wrapped them around her sister's wispy skull, curving them securely around her ears. Nell's eyes, immense now, focused on Rosalind.

"Lydia's sent you some potion the doctor wants you to have." Eileen poured a dose into a small glass on the bedside table, raised her sister's head, and held the glass to her lips. Nell made a sour face, but swallowed it.

"You'll be wanting the teeth," Eileen shouted, setting the medicine glass down.

Ros watched in horror as the bedridden old woman reached out, clawed the bedside table, contacted the teeth, and, with an immense effort, stretched her lips out of the way to allow her pale upper gums to receive the choppers. Ros tried to back out of range, but Eileen gripped her firmly.

Nell wheezed, "They told me . . . better not to mention it. Your mother said, I don't want her told . . . oh, it was a while ago now." The old woman closed her eyes.

Ros allowed herself to breathe, hoping she'd drifted off to sleep. Or died.

But Nell's eyes opened again. "Has it started, then?"

"Wh-what?"

"Do you see . . . patterns in things? Do you get a feeling for the future?"

"No!" Ros said sullenly. Her mother had been right; this was no fit place to be. The smell of the old woman's breath made her queasy. Under the bed she had noticed a chamber pot. Even with its lid on, she could smell that, too.

Eileen prodded her. "Speak nicely, girl, and speak up. Nell's hard-of-hearing."

"No, I don't!" Ros hollered.

Nell's eyes bore into hers. "Little liar! I can see by your face it's been given to you. You've the gift, just as my mother had. You are your great-grandmother all over again."

Ros stood rooted, repulsed, enthralled. Too hot, she undid her coat.

Eileen hissed in her ear, "She's been wanting to tell you about our mother, your great-grandmother, so you listen. Practicing it for years, just for you."

Why me? she wanted to say. Her shoulders sagged. She listened as the old woman's voice wheezed over sentences repeated so often they had the cadence of a chant.

"She was a comfort to all who knew her," Nell rasped. "Come from far and wide . . . Sir John A. himself, even . . . and kept herself and all us youngsters by telling people's fortunes . . . twenty-five cents a fortune, I believe it was. More for lost objects. And solved a murder, so she did . . . and went to watch the man hang."

The hook was baited; Ros listened.

Sucking her teeth tightly into her gum, Nell said, "Irish she was, the seventh daughter of a seventh daughter. And a proud man was her father, an officer in the British Army." Perhaps it was the effect of the medicine, but Nell's voice flowed now, like a spill of satin ribbon.

"As the child grew, she was deemed prettier than all her sisters, with eyes that would catch you and hold you and probe you. In all of Ireland, there was no match for the girl in beauty and wisdom. And her wisdom was uncanny and her mother feared for her, for she had the gift of foresight, which could bring her much pain.

"And fair of hair she was with coal black eyes and she danced every dance at all the balls. And it happened, at last, that she danced her way into the heart of a lowly young sergeant in her father's company." Nell moistened her lips with her tongue. "But her father forbade the marriage, and so it came about that the two eloped to Canada, and my poor mother was cut off from the family who had loved and nurtured her." The old woman's voice fell silent.

"Is that the end?" Ros felt cheated. Surely there was more. Nell's breath came in long snores, as if she had fallen asleep. Timidly, Ros reached out and touched her shoulder. With a shuddering sigh, Nell again took up the tale.

"At length my mother arrived on the shores of this very lake and made her home in a humble log house. And time passed, and soon it became known that my mother possessed powers beyond all understanding. And oh, they came from far and wide. When to plant the crops, they asked her, where to find lost items, and what would be the sex of their unborn child.

"And my father soon tired of the visitors and of his wife's gallivanting about the neighborhood and, although he forbade her to continue, he could not control her ways. He was not a man to be guided by a woman, and so he left her, and all of us children. He was a good-hearted man, but sorely tried.

"And 'twas no time at all before word got round that our mother could read teacups with the skill of the Delphic Oracle, as she came to be called. And I'd see how she'd swirl the teapot and give the leaves a good shake-up. And then must her fortune-seeker pour out a cup and carefully return the tea to the pot, making sure the leaves remained behind in the cup. 'Now turn it over,' she'd say, 'and twirl it.' And at last she'd pick up the cup and read it.

"And once, I recall, she turned the cup back over. A young girl sat before her. I saw my mother's face cloud. Her eyes, always bright as jet, grew dull; she didn't speak. At length, she handed the girl back her coin and said, 'I do not see a future in your cup.' And the girl looked down all sorrowful and embarrassed, as if she'd done a wrong thing, and my mother accompanied the girl to her waiting buggy and told the driver, 'Take the long road home, lad.' But he laughed and my mother stood in the road and watched them drive off.

"And on their way back home, less than an hour later, the young girl was thrown from the buggy and killed in an instant, for the horses took fright from a passing train."

Great-Aunt Nell's lips smacked closed and then open as she tried to moisten them with her tongue.

Ros waited, unable to take her eyes off the old woman's face.

Nell took a long breath. "And so it came about that my mother repeated to all those awaiting their turns, 'I can see no future.' And sadly she went back into the house and admitted no one else for many days to come."

Rosalind felt a chill and shivered. "And then what?"

Nell turned toward her, surprised. "Eh?"

"Wh-what happened next?"

Nell fixed her eyes on Rosalind's. "There was some called her witch. They used to burn witches." Her labored breathing filled the room.

Ros's voice was shrill with fear. "And was she?"

Nell wheezed, "And they'd call her in for the birthing of babies. And for the laying out of the dead."

"Was she?" Rosalind said, louder.

The old woman's voice faded to a whisper. "And she was the seventh daughter of a seventh daughter."

She reached out a frail hand toward Rosalind – its veins miniature purple mountain ranges, its tendons a fan of straight roads through them. "I put this story in your charge," she whispered, "because you're the one." Her dry fingers closed around Rosalind's sweaty hand. "You've been given it."

Rosalind ran, stumbling against furniture. Howling, she fled the house. Lucy flew down the stairs, following her out the door. "Little sister! Little sister!" Rosalind heard, as she ran onto the ice. Buttoning her coat, she looked back. For the space of three heartbeats they stared at each other. She knew, now.

She followed the red petals of Corny's blood in the snow. She thought they grew bigger as she passed – splashes, pools. Omens. She was nearly home before Corny, with his questions, caught up.

"Nothing," she answered. "Just some story." She turned to him, eyes bright as jet.

Dream Girls

Gillian Chan

I didn't actually meet Sonia Elliot until I was ten, but I had hated her for two years before that.

The year that I was eight, my mom had gone back to her hometown to visit Grandpa. Sonia lived in that town. She was the daughter of Mom's best friend in high school, and she was three months older than me.

According to my mom, Sonia was everything a girl should be – dainty, and a real little lady. She liked to wear the dresses her mother picked out for her, and have her hair fixed in fancy styles. She was always polite to adults and made an effort to talk to her mother's friends whenever they stopped by for a visit.

These Sonia stories really ticked me off because, although Mom never actually said it, I knew that she was thinking *not like you*. I mean, I didn't set out to disappoint her deliberately; it was just the way I was. Being thin and lanky like my dad, I looked like a jerk in the dresses Mom wanted me to wear. They were always made of material that itched and they showed my knobby, grazed knees.

I didn't see what was wrong with the clothes I liked. Pants in the winter and shorts in the summer were practical, especially if you spent most of your time outside, joining in whatever game was going on.

That was another thing that we didn't agree on. Mom thought I should spend more time indoors, doing quiet things, and less time with Ella Bean, whom I'd finally succeeded in making my best friend.

The summer I was ten, Mom went to visit Grandpa again. I dreaded her coming back because, at Ella's urging, I'd convinced my dad to let me have my hair cut short. He gave me the money without asking any questions. I felt kind of mean because I knew that he'd get into trouble too. But Ella and I headed into Elmwood and, instead of going to Lilian's where Mom always goes, we went to the town barbershop and per-suaded Mr. Mason to give us boy-type haircuts. I was expecting a real explosion when Mom saw me.

It never came. Mom came home with news. As her car drew up, Dad and I went out to meet her. I couldn't stop my hand straying to the satisfying sandpapery feel of my head. Mom gave a double take when she saw me, but then she sighed and told us her news: Sonia Elliot was coming to stay.

This was awful.

Later I just had to ask her, "Why is Sonia coming here?"

"Well, Dee Dee, her mother's not been very well. She's really run-down and could use a rest. So I suggested that while her parents went away, Sonia could come and stay with us for a couple of weeks. They jumped at the idea. I was a little surprised that they were so enthusiastic, especially as you and Sonia have never met." She smiled at me. "Anyway, it'll be nice for you to have someone to play with, won't it, sweetie?"

I could see Mom was going to love having Sonia around, being how Mom thought a girl should be. Mom had already made it pretty clear what she thought of Ella and her family. If Sonia were here, I wouldn't be able to spend so much time with Ella.

Ella and I had been planning, with her brother Jud, to build a fort out at the town dump, near where Ella lived. I knew that, even if I did get to go out, I'd almost certainly have to take Sonia with me. From Mom's description, I knew that Ella would think of Sonia as a real girlie-girl. With both wanting to be tough and as much like Jud as we could be, a girlie-girl was the ultimate insult. My new friendship with Ella might not survive a test like this.

"When's she coming? Exactly how long is she staying? Will she be sharing my room? Do I have to take her with me when I go out to play?"

Mom's sweet, patient answers made me feel mean for even asking. "Now, Dee Dee, I think you can be a bit more charitable. It can't have been easy for Sonia with her mother sick. I'll be relying on you to make her feel welcome. You think you can do that for me, sweetheart?"

"I s'pose so."

Mom drove me crazy all week with preparations for our little guest, as she called Sonia. My room was a major problem. Mom used Sonia coming as an excuse to get me to throw stuff out.

Then there was the matter of clothes. After huge arguments, she gave in and said that I didn't have to wear dresses the whole time Sonia was here, but I most definitely had to have a new dress to greet her and in case we went out somewhere fancy. The dress was pink, with tiny pearl buttons. It had stiff white crinolines that made its skirt stick out, so that I looked like a powder puff on thin stork legs. The worst thing was the hair bow – a fat satin one that perched on my head like a pink crow on a field of mown corn.

Sonia arrived with her father. He seemed eager to get away as quickly as possible, but Mom persuaded him to stay for tea. Sonia and I eyed each other like two cats.

"Sonia, honey, you don't know how pleased we are to have you stay with us. This is Della and I just know that you two are going to be good friends." She shoved me between the shoulder blades with a sharp knuckle. "Della, why don't you take Sonia to your room and get to know each other? You can show her where every-thing is."

Once we got to my bedroom, I was able to look at Sonia more closely. She was as pretty as Mom said, small and neat-looking. She reminded me of one of those fancy china dolls that you're never allowed to take out of the box. Sonia stared back at me without saying anything and then started to unpack her suitcase.

I thought I'd better make the first move. "My mom called me Della down there, but I prefer to be called Dee Dee."

"So?" Her voice had changed. It wasn't the sweet one she'd used downstairs.

"I just thought, if we are going to be friends, you'd like to know, that's all."

She looked straight at me then, her face blank. "I don't want to be here. I don't know you and, looking at you, I don't think I want to know you. What kind of girl has a boy's haircut?"

I was so shocked that I just stared at her.

"It's all your mother's fault. We were going to go to the lake and she convinced them that my mother would get more rest if it were just her and Dad. I wouldn't have been any trouble. And now I'm stuck in this dump, Elmwood, with you."

I couldn't let that pass. "Elmwood's OK. We can go swimming at the creek and I'll take you to meet my friend Ella."

"Hick stuff. Ella and Della, hick names, too!" Her laugh was mean. My joke with Ella, the rhyme our names made, turned into something babyish and silly.

I knew then that the next two weeks were going to be awful. And there were definitely two Sonias. Downstairs, she was all smiles and her voice was sweet.

"Dee Dee is so kind, Mrs. Carson. She said she'd take me to meet her friends and that you'd be taking us shopping."

Her father looked at her sharply. "You make sure you're on your best behavior, Sonia."

That was how it was. The nice Sonia turned up when my mom was around, but when we were alone, she was downright nasty. I tried telling Mom, but she laughed at me. "I just can't believe you, Dee Dee. Sonia's always so polite. Anyway, why would she be mean to you?"

"Because she hates it here, and she hates you for persuading her parents to go away by themselves."

"That's enough, Della Jane Carson. Now I know you're making things up because Sonia's told me how much she likes it here. I think you're jealous of all the fuss people make about her."

There didn't seem any point in trying again after that. Mom was having such a good time taking Sonia out shopping and to visit with her friends. I trailed along, hating the dresses Mom made me wear, wishing I was down at the dump with Ella.

I hadn't seen Ella for a whole week and it was driving me nuts. But, one day, Mom went to visit in the next town and said I could invite another friend over. Trudie, our cleaner, was to keep an eye on Sonia and me. Mom agreed when I said that I wanted the other friend to be Ella.

When Sonia heard, her face wrinkled into a sneer. "Ella? Ella Bean? Your mom's told me about her. She lives down by the dump, doesn't she? I bet she smells."

"She does not! She's my best friend. She makes up the best games and her brother Jud says she's the fastest pitcher he knows, boy or girl."

"Yeah, well, she sounds like a freak to me. But only a freak would want to be friends with you. You look more like a boy than a girl half the time. I can see why your mom gets so fed up with you." Sonia smiled as she saw tears well up in my eyes. It hurt that Mom had talked to Sonia about me.

There was a *rat-a-tat-tat* on the door then, the one that Ella and I used as our signal. She was standing on the porch grinning, hands stuffed into the pockets of shorts even older and scruffier than mine.

"How ya doing, Dee Dee? Jud and I have missed you."

I was so happy to see her. "I'll be back out at the dump with you next week."

Sonia had come up behind me and was staring over my shoulder. "So this is the great Ella, is it? I was right about why you two get on so well. You are a pair of freaks."

With one strong tanned arm, Ella pushed me out of the way and moved towards Sonia. "Well, it's better than being a two-bit girlie." Ella said this quietly, but I knew that I had to act fast because she was likely to take a swing at Sonia.

"Hey, what shall we do today?" My voice sounded bright and false.

Ella looked at me. "You said on the phone that we have to stay by the house so Trudie can keep an eye on us. There's not much we can do, right?"

"What about playing baseball cards?" Ella and I both loved baseball.

"That's boring," said Sonia. "I don't want to do that."

Ella looked at her. "Who cares what you want to do!"

"Ella, we can't leave her out. She'll tell on us when Mom gets back."

Ella grinned. "Who said anything about leaving her out?"

"I don't want to play baseball cards." Sonia's voice was whiny, "I want to play dress-up."

I was stuck in the middle. "Let's play both."

Ella and I sorted our cards, carefully putting aside the ones that were too good to play with. I loaned Sonia some so that she could play, too. The game was flipping cards against the wall, landing them on your opponent's cards to win them. Sonia wasn't much good and swore it was an accident when she used some of my best cards and they got bent.

Dress-up was just plain dumb. "I don't have any dressing-up clothes," I told Sonia.

She smiled. "We can use your mom's. She won't mind."

I wasn't too sure about that, but I reckoned that if we left everything as we found it, she'd never know.

Sonia tried on lots of Mom's clothes and got mad when we wouldn't join in. I was scared that she'd make a mess, especially when she started in on Mom's makeup. Ella just lounged against the wall, looking bored. When Sonia showed no signs of wanting to stop, Ella and I left her to it and went downstairs to wait for lunch.

All through lunch, Sonia kept smirking at us as if she had some kind of secret, but she left us alone in the afternoon. While we pitched to each other in the backyard, she sat on the swing and read Mom's magazines.

Ella had gone by the time my parents got back. "Did you girls have a good time? Trudie left no notes of complaint, so you can't have been any trouble."

In her sugary voice, Sonia said, "We had a lovely time, Aunt Jennie, didn't we, Dee Dee?"

I wondered why she wasn't telling Mom how Ella and I had kind of left her out.

"That's good to hear. I thought you might find Ella a little rough. Now, I think I'll go and change." Mom was upstairs for only a minute before she came running back down, shouting and shaking with anger.

"How dare you? You girls have been in my room, going through my things!"

Dad said, "Calm down, Jennie. I'm sure there's an explanation."

Mom ignored him. "And if that's not bad enough, you've poured perfume and powder all over my new satin comforter. It's ruined! Who did this?"

I started to explain but Sonia interrupted, her voice low and steady, "It must have been Ella. She was up there a while by herself when Trudie called Dee Dee and me to help lay the table for lunch."

I couldn't help it. I burst into tears. "That's not true! It was Sonia who was up there alone!"

"Della, stop making that dreadful noise," Mom said, staring at me. "I know Sonia well enough to know that she wouldn't do anything like this, but Ella – she's wild. . . ."

"Mom, please listen."

"No, I've heard enough lies from you about Sonia. Just go to your room." She didn't see the sideways look that Sonia gave me as I stood and headed upstairs.

The remaining three days of Sonia's visit dragged by. Mom barely spoke to me except to tell me what to do, or to make remarks about Ella. But Sonia was the worst. Whenever Mom was nearby, she acted like I was the best friend she had in the whole world.

When Sonia's dad arrived to take her home, Mom cried. My eyes were dry as stone.

"Oh, John, it's been such a pleasure to have Sonia here. She's any mother's dream – polite, helpful, and so charming." Not seeing the puzzled look that Sonia's father gave her, Mom carried on, "I do hope you'll let her visit us again. You will come, won't you, sweetie?"

Sonia smirked at me. "I'd like that. I had a really great time."

As we walked behind the grown-ups to the car, Sonia and I were silent. I had nothing to say to her.

I couldn't even smile when I heard her father quietly say to Mom, "We can't thank you enough for having Sonia. It was a real break for Carol. She and I were just wrung out. I wish Sonia were more like Della, and not so demanding and difficult."

The Thunderbird Swing

Nancy Hartry

Uncle Ted said Jimmy bumped his head falling off the swing. He said Jimmy just seemed to let go of the chains and, when he reached the highest arc, he fell, *thunk*, to the ground and lay still. Uncle Ted got out of his car and ran over to Jimmy. He said he talked to him. "Jimmy. Jimmy, wake up!" He slapped Jimmy's face. He jiggled him. When Jimmy didn't wake up, Uncle Ted carried him to the car and placed him gently on the backseat of his Thunderbird convertible. He didn't even stop to open up the door.

The last part is right. The getting out of the car, the talking, the slapping, the jiggling, the carrying, and even the laying down. The first part is not.

Jimmy never fell off the swing.

It was dim in the park when it happened. The street-lights had come on above the ravine, signaling all the little kids to leave. It was too early for lovers, and all the cigarette-puffing teenagers were at a community dance. Uncle Ted chose the perfect time to teach Jimmy a lesson he'd never forget.

Uncle Ted must have thought he'd get rid of the remaining kids by paying them off. He'd snapped a blue five-dollar bill over his head, folded it lengthwise, and passed it to Betty Lou, the tallest kid. "You're the banker, my dear. Off you go, and mind the little ones don't push and shove at the Dairy Bar."

Uncle Ted just didn't count on me, Cyndy, perched in a tree where the park and the parking lot meet.

It started at the beginning of the summer of 1958, on the last day of school. It was a Thursday. I know this because it was Uncle Ted's regular visiting night at his sister's house. Uncle Ted had made it his habit to visit Aunt Jean each Thursday ever since her eldest son, a fighter pilot, had been shot down over the English Channel in the war against Germany.

Just to be perfectly clear, I call them Aunt Jean and Uncle Ted, but they aren't my real relatives. Jimmy and I were born ten days apart. Aunt Jean is his mom and they live in the other side of my duplex house, which is the end one before you go down into the park. My bedroom and Jimmy's are separated by a fire wall. When we were little, we used to do Morse code messages on the wall after "lights-out," until Aunt Jean would scream, "Stop that blooming racket!"

So, since I've been born, I've spent more time in Jimmy's house than my own. My mom works crazy shifts at the button factory. Aunt Jean gets paid to watch me.

On the last day of school, a Thursday like I said, Uncle Ted parked in front of Aunt Jean's duplex house. All the kids streamed out of their houses, like ants to a honey pot, to see Uncle Ted's honey of a brand-new car. A baby blue and white Thunderbird convertible, with fins like wings.

Every kid in the neighborhood coveted that car, but no one more than Jimmy. All summer long, twenty times on Thursdays, Jimmy would say to me, "*Yippee,* it's Uncle Ted Day. Don't you love that car, Cyndy? Wouldn't you love to drive that car more than anything in the world?"

Boys are so dumb about cars. I could have said, "Jimmy, you need a license to drive a car." Or, "Jimmy, you have to be sixteen to drive a car!" But what was the point? I ignored him.

Every Thursday during the summer, while Uncle Ted was visiting with Aunt Jean in the back kitchen, the kids swarmed the car. They jumped on the bumper.

They took little kicks at the whitewall tires. They opened the doors, or slid over the doors and fell, *plop*, onto the white leatherette seats.

Some kids adjusted the radio or the aerial, but it was only Jimmy who sat behind the wheel. After all, Uncle Ted was Jimmy's uncle, so he should be the driver. Once Jimmy slipped on Uncle Ted's white gloves, no one asked him for a turn. He put on Uncle Ted's white driving cap backwards because the peak blocked his vision.

"*Rummmn. Rummmmn!*" Jimmy turned an imaginary key. All the passengers ran their engines too. I did the running commentary, telling them what we were passing. Steed's Dairy. Bush Hardware. Armitage's Bakery. All the sights up and down King Street. We acted like a bunch of five-year-olds.

Then Jimmy always got carried away. He tooted the horn at the Ye Olde Candy Store.

Uncle Ted would burst out of Aunt Jean's house, hollering. "You kids get away from my car! How many times do I have to tell you?"

The kids scuttled like cockroaches back to their duplex houses. Then it was only Jimmy, Uncle Ted, and me.

Uncle Ted shook his fist at Jimmy. "And to think I put you in charge!"

He turned to me. "How could you let him do it, Cyndy?" He handed each of us a chamois and we spent the rest of his visiting time polishing kid fingerprints off that car.

"It's not much of a punishment, is it, Cyndy?" Jimmy grinned so wide, I thought his mouth would reach his sticky-outy ears.

I do admit, now, that I liked the polishing. When you thought you were done and looked at the paint sideways, there'd be just one more print. I liked huffing my breath on the baby blue paint and then polishing the marks away. It was a challenge.

Each week the routine was the same. When Uncle Ted left, he kissed Aunt Jean good-bye. He peeled a purple ten-dollar bill from his billfold and pressed it in her hand. We gave him back the chamois. He patted my head and punched Jimmy in the right shoulder.

Although Uncle Ted Day was the most exciting day of the week, Fridays were a close second because we had group lessons at the community pool.

"What's that on your shoulder?" I asked Jimmy one Friday.

"Just a bruise. I must have fallen."

He couldn't fool me. That bruise on Jimmy's shoulder was an Uncle Ted Bruise. Each week it got darker and darker, one bruise on top of the last week's one, on top of the one from the week before, none of them getting a chance to heal between visits.

"Uncle Ted shouldn't hit you so hard."

"He doesn't mean anything by it. I'm just a softy, that's all. And he's like a big door. He doesn't know his own strength."

I squinted at Jimmy. That last part sounded like Aunt Jean's words. *Hogwash!* Uncle Ted may have been as tall and as wide as a door, but he was more like a screen door to my way of thinking. There was always hot air rushing out of him.

The Thursday before school went back in, the one before Labor Day, was Aunt Jean's summer windup canasta tournament. But she was prepared to stay home and visit with Uncle Ted like usual.

"Go. Go. Jimmy and I will be fine," said Uncle Ted. He gave Jimmy a little love-punch in the shoulder to prove it.

Don't go, Aunt Jean, I wanted to scream. *Stay home!* No words came out.

Aunt Jean put on her white gloves. She pinned her straw hat on her head and snapped her purse shut. She kissed Jimmy good-bye.

"Be good," she said, including me.

When Aunt Jean was almost out of sight, Uncle Ted turned to me and said, "Go tell your mother she wants you." So I went and sat on my porch.

"Jimmy, keep your little friends away from my car." He took the paper and sat in Aunt Jean's back kitchen, where it's cool and he could read in peace.

The kids swarmed all over the car as usual, but with Aunt Jean gone, Uncle Ted seemed madder. I think now that his anger had been building up each week for the whole summer.

When Jimmy tooted the horn, Uncle Ted came out screaming. Even I was scared and I was not involved. He yanked Jimmy out of the car and jumped in behind the wheel. Jimmy threw himself across the trunk.

"Get off. Get off, you kids." Uncle Ted started the engine. "I'm putting this car in gear." The car moved forward with a jerk. Then he slammed on the brakes. Forward, *slam*. Forward, *slam*, like a baby blue bucking bronco, until all the kids, laughing, fell off the car and onto the road. All except one.

Jimmy was splayed over the trunk holding on to a handle in the backseat.

Uncle Ted zoomed off down the lane into the park, with Jimmy bouncing on the back. All the kids followed.

I ran as fast as I could. My hair streamed off my neck and I galloped, trying to go faster.

When I got down into the park, the light was getting dim. The swings and the cat-poop sandbox and the picnic tables looked soft. Uncle Ted was blowing hot air about how rich and important he was and handing Betty Lou a five-dollar bill.

I shinnied up a tree and blended in with the leaves.

When all the kids were gone, Uncle Ted turned to Jimmy. He punched him in his sore shoulder and then his good shoulder and then his sore shoulder. "So you want to drive my car, do ya? Huh? Huh?"

Jimmy kept moving back during the punching and going forward to say, "Yes, I want to drive your car!" From my perch, it looked like they were doing the cha-cha dance.

Uncle Ted pushed Jimmy with two hands. "Well, you'll have to race me for it."

Jimmy got on his mark, lined up with the front bumper of the car. Uncle Ted tooted the horn and they were off. Uncle Ted gunning, gunning, and Jimmy pumping his legs so fast. He did pretty good. He ran straight down the parking lot. From my angle, I thought Jimmy won, but no, there had to be a rerun.

On the rerun, Uncle Ted changed the rules of the race. The car turned into a bucking bronco. It swerved into Jimmy's lane. It cut him off, just missing him.

Jimmy kept running. When he realized that Uncle Ted was chasing him, he sped up. Jimmy ran out onto the grass. Ted didn't care. He went up and over the log that marked the end of the parking lot and drove on the grass, trying to run Jimmy down. Jimmy darted. He dodged. He leapt out of the way and dove into the backseat of the car.

I thought he was safe now. But no, Jimmy was like a burr to be shaken loose. The car lurched and Jimmy was thrown from passenger door to passenger door and back again. Oh, those sore shoulders!

I started to get down from the tree. "Stop! Stop! Stop!" I was dangling from the lowest branch when Jimmy's body flew out the back of the car. It arced in the air and dropped to the ground, *thunk*. Jimmy lay still.

The rest I already said. I can't tell it as fast as it happened.

Apparently Uncle Ted passed Aunt Jean coming home from canasta. Aunt Jean tells how she cradled poor Jimmy's head all the way to the hospital.

Jimmy didn't go to school on the day after Labor Day. He hasn't been to school yet because of his head injury.

*

Uncle Ted still comes on Thursdays, which is fine because Aunt Jean has no other visitors but me, and Jimmy is a peck of trouble. A peck of trouble. Aunt Jean says that a visit from her only living relative makes a nice break. It's something to look forward to.

It is now my job to scoot the kids away from the car, which is easy because I have a new technique.

"Can Jimmy drive your car?" I ask Uncle Ted sweetly. "Those diapers he wears since he fell off the swing and hurt himself don't leak a bit."

Uncle Ted always lets him, but I have to put down the car blanket first. Jimmy sits behind the wheel and I go *rummmn, rummmmn.* He bounces up and down like a baby and the other kids stay away and watch.

When it's time for Uncle Ted to leave and he is handing over a ten-dollar bill, I say, "Aunt Jean could do with some more handkerchiefs because of Jimmy's drooling on account of his head injury from falling off the swing."

Uncle Ted peels two more bills off his billfold and presses them into Aunt Jean's hand. Then Uncle Ted goes to pat Jimmy on the head. Jimmy ducks. He tries to give me a love-punch in the shoulder. I put my two hands up like a shield and kick him in the ankle.

"Cyndy!" says Aunt Jean.

I don't say anything. What would be the point?

On Monday, Tuesday, Wednesday, and Friday after school, I push Jimmy on the swings. He loves to go really high and touch the sky.

Our Jimmy is not scared of anything or anybody. Neither am I.

Uncle Cory's Smile

Anne Gray

When I was a little girl, my uncle Cory used to hold me on his knee and read stories. He read our favorites over and over, as if he hadn't ever read them before. His broad finger moved slowly under each line, and he pronounced the words carefully, as if they were too precious to let go.

He helped me build towers from my blocks – high, high, higher than I could reach – and no matter how often I knocked them over, he laughed along with me. I rolled on the floor and giggled until I was breathless, and watched him grin. Then he would start to build again.

Red on blue, yellow on green. That was for me.

He liked purple on red, then yellow on blue, and I tried to build that, yet I could never get mine as tall as his. "But it's fine like that," he'd always say. "Never mind."

Sometimes, while we played, he would pat me on the head, and say, "I'm glad you've got blonde curls, just like your mom and me."

We played firefighters and pirates and astronauts. We crawled through a cavern made from a table and sheets. And when I asked if he would dress up, or play dolls with me, he always smiled his Uncle Cory smile, and said, "I'd like that fine."

When I got older, Uncle Cory taught me how to swim and ride my bicycle, carefully cleaning my skinned knees, and encouraging me to try again. He helped Dad build a tree house, and sewed yellow curtains along with me. My seams were pretty crooked, while his were neat and fine. We drew pictures for the walls – a squirrel, a giant bear, a tree. I drew one of him, and he drew one of me. He taught me how to bait a hook, and to wait patiently for something to bite. With our lines dangling in the water, we'd lie on our backs and look for animal shapes in the clouds.

If the evening weather was fair, Dad sometimes built a fire in the backyard. Uncle Cory and I roasted wieners and marshmallows, and we looked at stars. The stray black cat with fighting green eyes, which no one else could even touch, always curled up at his side and purred when he stroked her. When the fire had burnt low, with only glowing embers left, that's when Uncle Cory began to sing. His voice was so clear and sweet, it made me want to cry.

On my first day of school, Uncle Cory walked along with Mom and me, holding my hand. "Be sure you always look both ways," he said, "even when I'm with you." He glanced at Mom, a question on his face. She smiled and agreed, "Those are the rules."

After that, Uncle Cory took me to school each morning. "This is my best job," he'd say. After he dropped me off, he would go to his other job, in some kind of shop. "Just making things" was all he ever told me. But when school let out, he was always waiting, laughing and talking to the crossing guard, or one of the mothers. He seemed to be everyone's favorite.

"See you tomorrow, Cory," they'd call out, when we started to walk away. He was invited to all the parties, right along with me.

After school on Fridays, when I asked if he was ready to go for some chocolate chip ice cream, he smiled his Uncle Cory smile and said, "I'd like that fine."

Luci and Jen, my two best friends at school, soon became his best friends too, though at first Jen drew away, her brown eyes wide. "He is so big," she whispered, the first time she came to my house to play. "And it scares me when he frowns."

But he got those crooked lines in his forehead only when he didn't understand something, with his mouth pulled down and down. Usually when we had homework for school, he'd want to study with us, but he didn't seem to learn. He'd press his lips together and curl his hands into fists; I knew he was trying not to cry.

In the first and second grades, he kept up pretty well because he could read better than we could, but then the lessons got too hard. He looked so sad, playing alone in our backyard. As soon as we finished our homework, we'd go outside and dance around him, holding hands in a circle.

One day, when we got to school in the morning, I saw one of the new boys point at Uncle Cory. Standing beside them, three girls laughed behind their fingers, then elbowed each other and looked over my way, their eyes narrowed with glee.

Dummy, Dummy, has no brain.
Must have washed it down the drain.

The sharp-faced boy chanted it over and over, then others began to sing along, making funny faces.

Luci was standing near them. She looked a bit ashamed, but she didn't move off, or say anything to stop them. She just chewed on the ends of her hair and turned away. Then one of the other boys poked his tongue out of the side of his mouth, and paced around, his shoulders hunched.

I stood there, unable to move.

The first boy looked at me and grinned, all hard and mean. "Which would you rather have?" he called. "A nutbar or a fruitcake?"

"She's already got both rolled up into one," another boy yelled.

I looked back and saw Uncle Cory staring at them. Then he turned to me, his mouth gaping open, his eyes wide. I turned away and ran inside, even though I knew it would hurt him more than all those words. As I reached the door, I heard one boy call, "Aren't you going to say, 'Slow long'?"

All day I kept away from Luci, even though I could see that she wanted to get me on my own. I kept away from everyone, feeling frozen inside. My eyes ached from wanting to cry.

That afternoon, when I saw Uncle Cory talking with the crossing guard, I looked away. I heard him call my name, but I ran home alone. I didn't want to be seen with him, didn't want to hear the boys laugh or chant their rhymes, the way they had that morning. *Dummy, Dummy* burned on my brain.

When I got home, I went into my room and closed the door. I didn't want to be with Uncle Cory. I didn't want to see the question I knew would be in his eyes – a question I didn't want to answer, even in my own mind.

Maybe he didn't understand, I told myself; maybe he thought it was just a game. But I didn't really believe that, no matter how hard I tried. I threw myself on the bed, and wished that he was living somewhere else. I cried then, muffling the sound in my pillow. I didn't go to the door when Jen and Luci arrived, even though I heard Luci call out, "I'm sorry." I knew that she was crying too, but I didn't want to hear her excuses. I knew they were no better than mine.

When I went to the table that night, I wouldn't look at Uncle Cory. I didn't want to see his eyes. Mom and Dad exchanged puzzled glances, but said nothing, so I realized that Uncle Cory had not told on me for running home on my own, though he must have been frightened. After all, looking after me was his "best job."

We cleared the table and did the dishes, the way we always did, but he never said a word, and neither did I. Afterwards, he went to the corner of the den where we read and played, but he didn't ask me to join him.

That's when I knew for sure that he understood. My throat felt like I had swallowed a hard-boiled egg, shell and all. I watched as he pulled out those blocks we hadn't used in a very long time. He was fighting back tears as he slowly built a tower. Red on blue, yellow on green. He hadn't forgotten the colors for me.

I ran to my room, biting on my fist, and pictured those boys and girls at school, all cruel and cold. Heard them chant *Dummy, Dummy.* I thought of all the fingers pointing at Uncle Cory, then at me.

My own fingers seemed to point at me, too. I wondered if my eyes had also frozen him, and felt the shame grow. How could I have left him with those words still in his ears?

I looked out of my window, and saw the tree house in the light of the moon. I thought about the green-eyed cat, how gentle she had been with Uncle Cory. Uncle Cory had always sung my favorite songs first, while the embers of our fire still glowed. All that was worth facing down the ugly chants.

When I walked back into the den, the tower he had built was very high. Uncle Cory glanced up, then returned to his building. I sat down beside him, and began to build too.

Purple on red, then yellow on blue.

He watched my hands, and clasped his own in front of his chest, letting out a low sigh. After a while, I said, "Want me to read to you from my new book?"

He looked up, not quite sure.

"And tomorrow," I said, "on the way home from school, we'll go down to the ice-cream parlor and get some chocolate chip ice cream."

Uncle Cory went to bed happy that night, but I couldn't sleep, wondering what would happen when we got to school the next day. I thought how those boys would chant *Dummy, Dummy,* and wondered how I could face them.

I could be just as hateful. I could call out about elephant ears and potato noses and filthy clothes and stinky smells, and ask, "If you're so smart, why do you always fail your tests?" and then smirk. I tossed and turned all night, thinking of ugly things to say to the boys. And to the girls, too. That would make me as bad as they were, but what else could I do?

I was so sleepy in the morning, I could hardly eat breakfast. I could tell Mom was worried, and Uncle Cory, too. He whispered, "Do you want your mom to take you to school?"

I shook my head. "Unless you don't want to."

He swallowed hard. "That's my best job," he said.

I wasn't sure this was still true. As we walked, I realized I had to be as brave as he was, and not say the nasty things I'd planned.

My stomach churned as we got near to school, but I held my head up. The boys were waiting, and the girls, all grins and hugging their fists in their armpits.

Uncle Cory could have walked away; he'd done his job. But he stayed beside me. When the boys began to call, I almost forgot that I'd decided not to be mean; I almost said the meanest thing of all. I almost said, "If anyone cared about you, you wouldn't have to be so cruel."

But right now, I didn't care about them. I knew I'd have to face them another day, and probably another. Someday I might say words more spiteful than theirs, but I didn't want Uncle Cory to see me acting mean.

Luci and Jen stood off to one side, watching.

Uncle Cory squeezed my hand. I knew he was afraid, but he didn't run away. Not like I had yesterday. I squeezed his hand in turn. Then Jen and Luci walked over to Uncle Cory and me, and we all joined hands.

I knew then I could face the hateful words and nasty smirks. They didn't matter anyway.

Can You Keep a Secret?

Anne Laurel Carter

The year I turned five, I went to school dreaming I'd become a cowgirl. During the summer I'd seen a woman stand on a horse and ride bareback around a circus ring. Was school the wonderful place that would teach me how to do that? By nap time of the first day, I'd discovered that instead of riding lessons, I was expected to pretend sleepiness on a gritty rubber mat. The next thirteen years – save one – felt like a series of enforced naps in stuffy classrooms. Maybe it was because I grew up in a time and place where girls only dreamed of marriage, or – for better or for worse – of becoming nurses and teachers.

Whatever the reason, grade six stands out in my memory like the Rocky Mountains erupting from the flat concrete of my childhood Toronto. It was my one exciting year – until I turned seventeen and was finally old enough to escape into the world.

On the last day of June in grade five, I carefully ripped open my report card – addressed to my parents – on the walk home. I knew my mother was standing two blocks away at our kitchen door, waiting for it, but I bravely knelt on the sidewalk and ran the sharp edge of my ruler under its flap; the glue in my pencil case would be my accomplice in hiding my criminal act. I longed to get Mr. L. as my grade six teacher and I had to find out; he'd taught my older, smarter sister two years earlier and, ever since, he noticed me when he was on duty at recess. Though he asked, like everyone else, "Aren't you Lynn Ovenden's sister?" I didn't care that he didn't know my name. He'd smiled at me! His smile unblocked the auricles and ventricles of my heart – we'd studied the human body in health – and I was in a new world.

That day, looking at my report card, I died and went straight to heaven. There at the bottom was the name, *Mr. L.*, scrawled into the space announcing my class placement for September.

Mr. L. was the most handsome, intelligent, exciting man in Don Mills, probably on the face of the earth. His red convertible sat in the parking lot beside the subdued grays and blacks of the other cars. He often left the roof down and I'd walk past it, just to glance inside and smell the white leather seats. Lynn had told me the ages of his children and I'd hotly debated his age with her. His eldest son was eighteen. I was convinced Mr. L. couldn't be forty. That was too ancient for the prince of men. No. My idol must have married at eighteen – no, seventeen! – and by my calculations, he was barely thirty-five.

In September I ran to school to greet my first day of grade six. Mr. L. didn't disappoint me. He'd learned my name.

"Hello, Anne!" he said, and smiled. My heart pounded. "I hope you don't mind sitting in the back. I expect you'll be an excellent student, if you're anything like your sister. I like my best students in the back."

Usually I hated being compared to my older brother and sister. They'd mastered reading about Dick and Jane, riding a bike, and playing the piano before I even got a chance to begin. Whether it was the result of my parents' lack of imagination, the 1960s, or our middle-class suburb, I was put through the exact same paces they were, especially those of my sister: Anglican Church choir, a weekly lesson with Mrs. Nelson, the piano teacher on our street, and swimming lessons at the Don Mills pool on Saturday afternoons. In the Christmas pageant at church, my sister was Mary, Mother of God, and sang a solo; I was a silent angel scratching my halo. I painfully memorized "Home on the Range" for Mrs. Nelson's piano recital; Lynn whizzed through Beethoven's "Fur Elise" to a standing ovation. I struggled with the belly flop while Lynn perfected her swan dive.

The only thing I silently gloated over was that my sister didn't get to skip grade two. In grade one students learned to read endless, boring stories about Dick and Jane and their dog, Spot. If we could correctly answer skill-testing questions, we got to miss grade two – further adventures of Dick and Jane and their dog, Spot. Lynn had hepatitis, missed most of grade one, and wasn't allowed to skip a grade. I was.

So, would I sit in the back for Mr. L. and be an excellent student? I'd have sat outside looking in the window if he'd asked me. I'd show him a student like he'd never seen before. In grade six I wouldn't procrastinate. Up until then I had preferred playing outside to doing homework, but the minute Mr. L. handed out the first assignment, I went home and threw myself into the task.

Our first project concerned the early explorers and trade routes. I raided my mother's spice rack and sewing cabinet. I made little pouches of cinnamon and cloves and attached them to their source country on my hand-drawn map of the world. I sewed porcelain buttons and squares of silk and cotton between borders. Mr. L. had never seen anything like it. He asked me to give an oral presentation to the class. Skipping a year into a class of older kids had made me shy and self-conscious. My hands shook as I held my handmade map, but I kept my eyes on Mr. L., eager to win his smile.

In October he had to choose two students for a special enrichment class on Friday mornings. He announced the names before recess one Monday. Mine was one. My face fell and being the kind sensitive prince he was, he asked me to stay behind.

I was nervous.

"Something tells me you don't want to go, Anne. Am I right?"

I couldn't lie to him. I would *never* lie to him. I nodded.

"But why? She's a fabulous teacher. You'll learn so many things that I won't have a chance to teach this class. Geometry. A whole new system of counting called bases. You'll learn about great humanitarians. Have you ever heard of Albert Schweitzer?"

I shook my head. If Albert didn't live in Don Mills, I'd never heard of him.

"Don't you want to know about him?"

I thought about it. I did. But I shook my head. I admitted my reason. "I don't want to miss a minute of your class. This is my only year with you."

He studied me, choosing his words carefully. "Then do it for me. Try it. Try for a few weeks and if you don't like it, you don't have to go."

For the first time in grade six I dragged my feet to school on Friday, but it took only one enrichment class to hook me. I ran to school as usual after that, even on Fridays.

In the fall and spring of grade six he took us outside, where we were allowed to lie under a great oak tree. He leaned against the rundled trunk and read for hours from *Huckleberry Finn* and *Anne of Green Gables*. His voice was deep and wove a magic spell. I was a vivid daydreamer. I lost myself in those hours, living in the Deep South, or becoming a redheaded orphan on the green fields of Prince Edward Island.

I was vaguely aware he didn't smile at everyone, particularly the boys he placed in the front row. Will Fergus sat front and center before Mr. L.'s desk. He was a rough-and-tumble boy and his hands easily got dirty. If a page in his notebook got smudged after a recess of baseball or wrestling, Mr. L. saw nothing wrong with ripping it out in front of the class and tossing the crumpled work into the dark green garbage pail. I was vaguely aware this might not be the best year of Will's childhood.

I gradually lost my shyness and made friends. I wouldn't walk with Will Fergus when he waited for me outside, but he often chased me home. I secretly liked the breathless excitement of it, but I preferred a quiet boy, Derek Anderson, who sat beside me in the back. Derek's penciled sketches amazed me: pictures of his hands; my arm across my desk; or the back of Andrea's head in front of him, with wisps of hair escaping her fat braids. Mr. L. sometimes took us outside for art class and I made sure to sit beside Derek then. I didn't mind that Derek drew far better than me. He inspired me to draw a tree as it really looked: not my usual thick, straight trunk topped by a blob of green, but a trunk that curved and split off in three directions topped by unorganized branches. I'd learned in enrichment class that a mature oak tree could lose a quarter of a million leaves every fall, and I patiently dabbed hundreds of tiny green leaves of paint to represent them. I liked my picture; Derek smiled encouragement at me.

At some point during the first term of grade six, Mr. L. asked me if I played the piano as well as Lynn. "I'd like to have a talent afternoon at the end of June and wondered if you'd like to prepare something?"

I took a new shocking interest in my weekly lessons and actually began to practice. By spring, Mrs. Nelson had to speak to my parents. In six months I'd outgrown her skills; I needed a better teacher. At our Grade Six Tiny Talent Time, I played a Bach invention. Mr. L. gave me a standing ovation.

On the last day of grade six, Will Fergus rejoiced and I wept. My special year with Mr. L. was over. Nevertheless, I still had one thing to look forward to. Mr. L. and his wife owned a horseback riding camp and my parents had agreed, after much begging, that I could attend for two weeks that summer. Lynn had never gone; we always went to the Anglican Church summer camp, where Lynn was given the starring role in the camp musicals. She was Alice in *Alice in Wonderland*. I was the white rabbit who disappeared after scene one.

Ha, ha! Horseback riding would be mine, and mine alone. The circus was just around the corner!

I learned to groom horses and love the smell of a stable. I learned to wait patiently before tightening the saddle, until the horse gave up and let out his drawn breath. Although I didn't stand bareback on a horse, I learned to ride that summer and loved it.

After a day of riding, in the late heat of the afternoon, we used to all go to the river, taking turns to jump onto a tire suspended by a rope from an old willow tree's branch. The willow overlooked a steep bank above a curve in the winding river below. The water was deep and slow, but only the brave would sail out over the middle and flip off, spinning through the air for a long second before plunging into the dark water below with a splash. I went there every day until the last weekend, when Mr. L.'s eldest son came to visit with his girlfriend.

That girlfriend was gorgeous; she was well developed and wore the skimpiest bikini I'd ever seen. There was a pop song on the radio with a line about a teeny-weeny bikini and that became my silent nickname for her. Her dark hair was long and she constantly ran her fingers through it.

On my last Saturday afternoon at the camp, during quiet hour, I sneaked out to the swimming hole alone. We weren't supposed to, but after years of swimming lessons at the Don Mills pool, I was a good swimmer.

My year in grade six had increased my vocabulary. The river was as *languid* as the great Mississippi, seeking relief under the cool shadows away from the firey July sun. Without looking left or right, I made a run for the tree and the black rubber tire. I'd perfected my timing. I caught the bottom of the tire. It burned in my hands, but I clung to it anyway. My feet left the ground and I sailed through the air above the bank, out over water. I anticipated exactly the moment I'd reach the top of the arc, transcribed by the line of the rope – I'd learned geometry in enrichment class – and that was exactly when I let go.

It was also the moment I saw them. They'd been swimming together and were just leaving the water, about forty feet from where there was a small sandy beach. Mr. L. stood waist deep with his son's gorgeous girlfriend in his arms. I recognized the teeny-weeny bikini. Her face was turned away, pressed close to his in a passionate kiss. Her arms were wrapped around his neck. I didn't flip through the air, or somersault, or try a swan dive. I plunged, feetfirst, straight into the water. My feet touched bottom as my mind thrashed to review the picture. I'd obviously mistaken Mr. L.'s son for Mr. L. *Scary thought!* I kicked furiously and broke the surface, not needing air so much as the trusty lens of my safe, childhood camera.

I swam toward them, got a footing on the bank, and struggled closer until I stood only a few feet away. I'd learned the word *discretion* that year too, but its nuances were lost on me. I stared at Mr. L. and Teeny-Weeny, wiping water from my unbelieving eyes. My mouth flapped open like a fish desperate to go back home.

For the very first time, Mr. L. didn't smile at me.

"Can you keep a secret?" he asked. His voice had that threatening tone, the one he used with the boys at the front of the class.

I nodded.

"Then do."

I waded out of the water, struggled across the beach and began to run. The sun was hot, begging me to walk, but I ran up the bank. The long green grass was mottled with dried dirt and whipped lightly against my bare legs, leaving dusty traces.

At supper that night, our last night, Mrs. L. made apple crumble. My mother used to make it, too. It was my favorite dessert, but I couldn't eat. I couldn't look at him. His smile would mean nothing to me. I was secretly glad, when the time came for seconds, to hear Mrs. L. refuse Teeny-Weeny another helping, without offering an apology or explanation.

I turned twelve in September and went to a different school. In grade seven I bravely chose art as my optional course. At the end of the first class, the teacher walked around the room, behind us, to study how well we'd drawn the vase on the table. He stopped behind me.

"You obviously didn't see the guidance counselor. You picked the wrong option. Why don't you try sewing or typing instead?"

It would be another six years before I left Don Mills and dared to sketch anything again. During that time, whenever I saw a red convertible driving around Don Mills I glanced, but the driver always looked so much older – more like a hundred. By then, I'd made myself forget too many things: how his smile used to inspire me; and that I had a dream of riding horses bareback in the circus.

Tales of a Gambling Grandma

Dayal Kaur Khalsa

My grandma was a gambler. This is the story of her life as she told it to me and as I remember it.

Grandma was born in Russia. When and where exactly, she did not know. She only remembered that one night the Cossacks charged into her village, brandishing their swords and scaring all the people.

My grandma (who was only three years old) jumped into a cart full of hay and covered herself. Somewhere she lost her shoe. And so, she escaped to America wearing only one little black shoe, hiding in a hay cart drawn by a tired white horse, all the way across the wide, slate-green Atlantic Ocean. At least, that's how she told the story to me.

She landed in Brownsville, Brooklyn.

There she grew up.

When she was old enough to get married, my grandma borrowed a balalaika. She couldn't play the balalaika, but she could hum very loudly.

Every evening she sat down with her balalaika on the front steps of her building, trying to catch a husband.

One night, Louis the plumber, trudging home weary from work, saw her. She made such a pretty picture with her balalaika and her long golden hair and rosy cheeks that he dropped his heavy leather bag of plumbing tools – *clank* – and asked her to marry him.

And she, actually strumming the balalaika – *plink, plank, plunk* – said, "Yes."

And that's how our family began.

They had two children.

My grandpa got a job fixing the pipes in Dutch Schultz's hideout. Dutch Schultz was a big-time gangster, and though he broke the law a lot, he was very kind to my grandpa. He paid him lots of money and always gave it to him on time.

But good jobs like that were hard to find. To help make extra money, my grandma learned how to play poker.

She was very good – sharp-eyed and quick with her hands. She could mark a card with her fingernail and hide aces in her sleeve. And, most important, she liked to win. Wherever there was a hot card game going on in Brooklyn, my grandma was there – winning money.

Her children grew up.

Her son moved out to California. Her daughter (who was my mother) married a handsome man from Queens. They bought a brand-new house.

When my grandpa died, my grandma moved into their house in Queens. Then, I was born; a pink little girl for her to hug and squeeze.

My parents worked all day, so right from the start my grandma and I were always together.

We spent most of our time under the great weeping willow tree in our front yard. My grandma sat like a flowering mountain in her big green garden chair. All day long she knit scarfs and shawls and socks. She told me stories of her life and gave me two important pieces of advice.

One: Never, ever go into the woods alone because the Gypsies will get you or, should you escape that cruel fate, you'll fall down a hole.

Two: Just in case the Cossacks come to Queens, learn to say *"Da"* and always keep plenty of borscht in the refrigerator.

Whenever I had a cold, Grandma let me stay in her bed. She made a tent from a sheet and an overturned chair. All day long we kept busy together polishing pennies bright copper.

When I became bored with this, she'd slowly slide open her bedside table drawer.

I liked that drawer.

First there was the smell of sweet perfume and musty old pennies. Then there was a tiny dark blue bottle of Evening in Paris cologne, shaped like a seashell; a square snapshot of my grandma holding me as a baby; big, thick, wriggly-legged black hairpins; and stuck in corners so I had to use the hairpins to get them out, dull brown dusty pennies.

But most fascinating of all were my grandma's false teeth. I never saw her put them in her mouth. She always kept them in the drawer, or if she were going visiting, they stayed smiling secretly in the pocket of her dress.

My grandma let me touch everything, even the teeth.

And she'd promise if I would get better really fast, she'd take me somewhere.

To the midway at Coney Island.

To a vaudeville show, starring Rosie, the Beer-Drinking Hippopotamus.

To a movie that had the very same name as my grandma – *Anna*.

Or to a Chinese restaurant, where we drank tea in thick little cups.

Grandma had lived a very long time, she said, and she had learned a thing or two.

Sometimes, as I grew older, she would look at me in a certain way and say, "Let me give you a few friendly words of advice." This was always followed by what she called a Law of Life.

One law was all about how to draw people: Always color their cheeks bright pink and give them big red smiles so they look healthy.

Another law was about crossing your eyes: Don't – because the cords will snap and they'll stay that way forever.

And whenever I had a question but there was no answer right away, Grandma told me her very best Law of Life: "Don't worry. Sooner or later, for every pot there's a lid."

Most of our time was spent quietly under the willow tree, just the two of us. There were occasional visitors under our willow tree – other children in a quiet mood, the next-door cat on its way somewhere else, the mailman, and two tall nuns who lived around the corner.

And every Thursday afternoon the Sunshine Ladies came.

Grandma missed the excitement of her old gambling days, so she organized the other grandmas in the neighborhood into the Sunshine Ladies Card Club. They met in our backyard.

At first they played canasta just to win pennies. Then, to make it more interesting, my grandma suggested they play for what she called trifles – gold lipstick cases, compacts, pillboxes, charms, brooches, lockets – anything that was shiny and gold.

My grandma won everything.

Every year Grandma took a long train trip straight out across the country to California to visit her son. She traveled on the Santa Fe Chief. And that train was so luxurious, she said, that she spent the whole trip soaking in a big white tub full of fresh orange juice.

When she arrived in California, "Bright orange," she said, her son picked her up at the train station and brought her to his little pink stucco bungalow. He arranged a giant-sized, two-week-long poker game in her honor.

All his friends came. They played poker, chewed gum, ate potato chips, and drank celery tonic without end. My grandma had a wonderful time.

And she brought back a fabulous prize she had won in the poker game. It was a big bright shiny gold ring with two glittering diamond chips.

She let me hold the ring for a while and told me that when I grew up it would be all mine. Then she dropped the heavy ring into a little green velvet bag and put it in her bedside table drawer with the other treasures.

It was just around then that Grandma decided it was time for me to learn how to play cards. After supper one night Grandma cleared the dining room table quickly. She lined up little piles of pennies and set out a fresh deck of cards. She taught me how to play go fish, old maid, and gin rummy.

At first we played just to win those dusty pennies brought down from her drawer.

But after a few weeks of lessons, when I had learned how to hold my cards close to my chest so no one could see them, and to *not* bounce up and down yelling "Guess what I have!" every time I got a good hand, then she taught me how to play what she called *real* cards – straight poker, five-card stud, three-card monte, chicago, and blackjack.

Grandma kept using the old pennies from her drawer. I used my allowance. "To make it more interesting," my grandma suggested.

Grandma wiped me out.

Any part of my allowance that I hadn't lost playing poker, I put in a shoebox in the bottom of my closet. I was saving up to buy a Ping-Pong-Pow Gun, a giant plastic bazooka that shot real Ping-Pong balls.

I saved and saved and saved and at last I had enough money to buy the gun.

Grandma took me downtown to Macy's toy department. I rushed to the Ping-Pong-Pow display and grabbed a gun. My grandma picked up a pink-cheeked Betsy-Wetsy doll.

She had the same look on her face as when she had warned me about the Gypsies and the Cossacks and the holes. She looked down at my giant bazooka and slowly shook her head. "Let me give you a few friendly words of advice," she said. "Guns are for boys. Girls play with dolls. Buy the doll."

I had never disagreed with my grandma before.

But – a doll!

"No!" I said. "Anyone can play with anything!"

And that was the only real argument my grandma and I ever had.

Guess who won?

Every day I came home from school for lunch. Grandma sat waiting for me at the dining room table.

I only ate sandwiches that were cut into four long pieces with the crusts cut off. My grandma understood this because her favorite sandwich was a banana rolled up in a piece of rye bread. I never sat down to eat. Instead, while my grandma listened to the soap operas on the big brown radio, I marched around and around the living room rug, stepping only on the roses. Every once in a while, I'd make a loop into the dining room to take another tiny sandwich from my grandma's outstretched hand.

One day Grandma got sick. Her eyes turned bright yellow and my parents took her to the hospital.

When I came home for lunch the door was locked. A neighbor called to me, saying my mother said I should have lunch at her house.

I sat in a chair in her silent kitchen, with no soap opera, and ate a sandwich cut only in two. Then I went back to school.

When I came home at three o'clock the front door was open. I went into the house and into the darkened dining room. My mother was sitting at the table.

She said, "I have something very sad to tell you."

And I said, "Yes?"

And she said, "Your grandma died this afternoon."

And I said what I had heard other people say sometimes: "Oh, I'm sorry to hear that." And I went upstairs to my grandma's room.

I opened the drawer of her treasures and made sure that everything was there: the pennies, the bottle of cologne, the snapshot, her hairpins and false teeth, and the little bag with the ring.

Then I opened her closet door and stepped inside. I closed the door behind me and hugged and smelled all my grandma's great big dresses.

And that's the story of my grandma's life as she told it to me and as I remember it.

When I grew up, my mother gave me my grandma's gold and diamond ring. And though I found out that it wasn't made out of real gold at all and that the diamond chips were only glass, I wouldn't trade my grandma's ring for all the gold and diamonds in the world.

How It Happened in Peach Hill

Marthe Jocelyn

Mama told me to lie.

She said it would be best, when we got to Peach Hill, if I practiced the family talent of deception; I was likely to hear more if I appeared to be simple. So, I perfected the ability to cross one eye while my mouth stayed open. I breathed out with a faint wheeze so that my lips dried up, or even crusted. Once in a while, I'd add a twitch.

People would take a first look and shiver with disgust. Then they'd look again and think, *Oh the poor thing, thank the heavens she's not mine.* And then they'd ignore me. I got the two looks and became invisible. That's when I went to work. People will say anything in front of an idiot.

I gathered gossip and brought it home to Mama. She put it to use in little ways, giving it back to the very same people, only shaped differently and in exchange for money. Lots of money, over time.

I thought of us as gardeners. I prepared the soil; Mama decided on the arrangements and planted the seeds. The customers decided if it was flowers, vegetables, or weeds they were going to harvest.

That's the kind of thinking that floated through my brain while I was trying to act daft.

We arrived in Peach Hill toward the end of summer and there was not a peach tree in sight. There was a hill, though, dotted with fancy houses that might have had peach trees before they had swimming pools and rose gardens. We took a ground-floor apartment down in the town, knowing our stay would be temporary.

The front room, where Mama received company, was set up in the most careful and lovely manner. There was a cushy red armchair for the customer and a smaller one for Mama, with a polished table in between. An ivory lace curtain dappled the light and a sign in the window, lettered in pearly script, announced *Madame Caterina, Spiritual Advisor.*

Mama was sharp, I'll give you that. She was a fake as far as hearing from the dead, or even seeing the outcome of a situation ahead of time, but she had a sensitive way about her, when required professionally,

that drew out secrets. With a little background infor-
mation, she could easily appear to see straight into the
hearts of forlorn and desperate women – it was usually
women – who would spend heaps of money to hear the
advice of a stranger. While she seemed to be reading a
palm, she examined the watch and assessed the jewelry.
Certain services were offered when the rings had bigger
stones. Services that cost a little more.

Mama claimed we had Gypsy blood, that wanderlust
and fortune-telling came naturally. But she also prom-
ised me we were getting rich and that, someday soon,
we could buy a house all of our own.

Peach Hill was our sixth town, Mama's and mine. It
didn't take long for word to flutter around like a flock
of birds. People might scorn us in public, but nearly
everyone had a reason to seek us out on the quiet. The
women were quickly convinced that Mama had the
second sight, the things she knew.

My acting daft seemed to be working. The main
benefit for me was that schools don't take loonies, so
I was off the hook for education as far as Peach Hill
was concerned. The downside was that I had no friends.
Who would be friends with a wonky-eyed, chapped-
lip moron?

After a few days of experimenting, I pinpointed the
two best places in town for eavesdropping: the benches

in the square, out front of Bing's Café, or one of the shaky wooden stools at the Cosmos Launderama.

We hired what Mama called a girl, though she must have been nearly twenty. At first I thought she was as slow as I pretended to be, the way she shook her head from side to side while Mama gave instructions. Then I realized she just couldn't control her disbelief at the things asked of her. Mama always tossed in extras so that Peg would have something to whisper about.

"Leave the pillowcases inside out on the beds, Peg. Makes the spirits restless and readier to communicate."

"Yes'm."

"We'll need fifty-two mushrooms, with the stems at least two inches long. And a new deck of cards."

"Yes'm."

"And Peg?"

"Yes'm?"

"Call me Madame, Peg. Not 'Yes'm.' I'm a clairvoyant, not a butcher's wife."

"Yes'm."

And off went Peg, head swaying.

"What are we going to do with fifty-two mushrooms?" I asked.

"Sauté them and eat them on toast during Peg's day off." Mama winked at me.

I didn't have friends, but I knew the name of every kid in town. That's not bragging; that's collecting data. I had a tiny notebook especially adapted. One of those little diaries that six-year-olds have, with a pony on the cover and a slim gold pen attached in a snug leather loop. I hammered a hole through the top of the spine and it hung around my neck on a length of blue ribbon.

I worked out my own code. The townspeople thought it was part of my disability, the way I'd coo like a dove and scribble marks in my book.

"Do you suppose she thinks she's writing poems?" I heard Mrs. Ford say to Mrs. Romero. "Poor thing, she sees the other children with their schoolbooks and wants to be the same."

Ha. Ha-ha-ha.

No, Mrs. Ford, I was making a note to tell Mama about the letter you received from your husband's ex-wife. And she'll hear about your unhappily married daughter, Mrs. Romero, because nothing is better for business than misery and longing.

But, I would think to myself, *you can cluck your tongues if it makes you feel better, and I'll just make my doodles.*

It was harder to sit near the kids. Kids do not welcome idiots into their circle and they either chased me with stones and nasty names, or slunk off to a place I couldn't follow. But, after a time, they got used to me.

They could see I was only stupid and harmless. They finally ignored me, just like their parents.

There was one boy, named Sammy Sanchez. They always called him Sammy Sanchez, as if there were other Sams he might be confused with. Not a chance. I might as well say it – he was the most wonderful boy I ever saw. He'd been away at his aunt's farm for the summer and the first time he showed up in the square, I forgot myself and stared with both eyes, looking straight at him. Of course he was not looking at the loony girl and nobody else was either, so I could have blown him a kiss and not been caught. But I didn't. I recovered myself and stumbled off my bench with hot cheeks. I heard a ripple of choked-back laughs as I loped home, looking as dim-witted as I possibly could.

Peg found me crying in the kitchen. I sobbed that they'd teased me, that I was ugly and wanted to die.

"Ah, now," said Peg. "There, there." She stroked my head and patted my back till I settled down. "You'd be quite pretty if you wore sunglasses. Never mind there's a vacancy between your ears. Try closing your mouth, if you can. And wash your hair once in a while, for pity's sake!" She had me lean over the side of the sink while she gave my head a scrubbing, and then doused it with something smelling of lemons.

Nearly all our patrons were female, as I said. We'd get the odd young man on a matter of romance, and one fellow, Bobby Pike, who begged Mama to help him bet on the horses. But, when Mr. Poole arrived, middle of September, along with golden light in late afternoons, we knew the season was changing in more ways than one.

Mr. Poole lived halfway up the hill, in a house with a lily pond, all wrapped round with a wrought iron fence. Mr. Poole fancied himself a very dapper fellow, and used an oil to sculpt his rippling gray hair that smelled like a sunny island. His wife, Mrs. Poole, had died a year ago, from an ailment that had her looking like a skeleton long before she passed. I knew this the same way I knew everything, from listening.

Mama didn't like me nearby when she was working, but I found a way around that. I inched the big chair in the front room into such a position that I could sit behind it with my knees scrunched up and my back in the crook of the wall.

Thanks to this, I knew from the start how things stood with Mr. Poole. He was certain that his wife had returned to haunt him. She didn't like the new crockery he'd chosen and she'd broken four teacups, jumping them off their hooks to the floor. She didn't approve of his putting new fish into the pond and she'd left two of them gasping on the bank. Mr. Poole wanted Mama to contact Mrs. Poole and tell her to stop.

"You remind her that I'm alive and she's not," he said. "I've been drinking out of teacups covered in primroses for twenty-two years and it's time for a change."

He was pretty ruffled. Mama soothed him into the big chair I was tucked behind and said she could see how important it was for her to reach Mrs. Poole.

"They usually respond quickly when they're upset," lied Mama, in her sweetest voice. "Though she'll expect a little coaxing to move on quietly. I can set up a 'calling,' but I'll need a cup of dirt from your garden and a small advance to pay for other particular materials. How would Friday night suit you?"

Friday would be just fine with Mr. Poole and out came his billfold, with Mama murmuring right next to him all the way to the shoe shop on the corner. I slipped to the window and saw him patting her arm more than once, he was that grateful. She came back humming and slid the dollars into her purse.

Mama wasn't the only one thinking about where a romance might lead.

I knew I had it bad the morning I got up early to

watch Sammy Sanchez walk past on his way to school. I'd figured out we were on the path from his house near the rail yards to the school at the bottom of the hill.

Sammy didn't wear a baseball cap like the other boys. His black hair flopped and blew in the autumn wind like . . . well, like shiny black hair. As the week ticked by, I got bolder with my spying. On Friday morning, I left the spot behind the lace curtain and moved to the doorstep. I put on Peg's sunglasses and tossed my hair. I was cheating on being daft, and Mama would likely strangle me if she knew.

I licked my lips and let them form a tender smile. Sammy Sanchez wheeled along on his skateboard and hopped off just as he came to the cracked sidewalk in front of our building.

"Hey," he said, maybe surprised for a second before he realized it was me. He gave me a wave and took two steps. Then *whoosh* – back on the board and he was gone. I about fainted. He'd spoken to me!

I was in heaven. And then immediately in the darkest pit. There is no wonderful, black-haired boy on earth who wants a wonky-eyed, chapped-lip moron for a girlfriend.

It was time to move on. I had to tell Mama. We were rich enough. We could find a little cottage in a town by the ocean, with a boardwalk and a concert in the bandstand on Sunday afternoons. I'd go to school with clean hair and have friends and find another boy.

But, at supper, Mama had something to tell me first.

"I like Peach Hill," she announced. "What would you think of moving into a house with a lily pond?"

"What?" I shouted. "No! We can't stay here! You think I want to be an idiot for the rest of my life?" I couldn't believe she would suggest such a thing.

"I'll not be hollered at by my own child," said Mama.

"You only ever think about you!" I got louder. "What about me?" I was mad as a trapped wasp.

Mama scraped back her chair and stood up, her hands clenched. "Calm down at once." Her voice had an edge like a cleaver. "Peg will be back any moment. You go to your room and settle down. I need you to help with the 'calling' for Mr. Poole's wife."

"Are you going to tell *Mrs.* Poole what your plans are? Why should you get to have a greasy-haired boyfriend while I'm the ugly duckling? You want me to drool and stammer at your wedding?"

Mama tried to freeze me with her gray eyes, but did not bother to speak. I ducked past her and headed for the door. Outside I could make the noises that expressed my feelings.

"Grrrack! Arrggerrack! Aarrrroooeeeeww!"

People stepped out of my way in a hurry. I'd have grinned if I weren't so mad. Nothing like a loony on a rampage to clear the path.

I stomped around the square a dozen times. The tears were pouring. Maybe I was crazy, after all, even having daydreams. I sat on the bench, hunched over, my elbows digging into my knees. I must have sat like that for an hour or more, still as the bench itself. Finally I noticed it was getting chilly. The heat was gone from my anger.

I knew Mama would be waiting. She couldn't do a proper séance without me there to knock on the walls and waver the lights. She'd be pacing, wondering if I was coming to help her trick old Mr. Poole. I was shuddering with leftover sobs when I finally trudged home.

"Ah, girlie," said Peg, when I came in. "Have those bullies been at you?" She wrapped her arms around me, warm as a blanket, making me cry all over again. Peg loved me, not knowing I was smarter than she was. She loved me because I was helpless. She loved me the way a mother loves a baby.

And speaking of mothers, "Where's Mama?"

"There now," said Peg, smoothing the hair away from my face. "She's in the front room, just finishing with

Mr. Poole." Then she giggled. "Though it looks more like a beginning, if you ask me." She giggled again.

I pulled out of the hug and gulped for air.

"She's *kissing* him?"

Peg peered at me, cupping my face in her rough hands.

"Your eye!" she whispered. "It's straight!"

Oh, skunk! I'd blown it. I thought for a second to fall down and pitch a scary fit, with my tongue hanging out. But then my chance for freedom flashed like sheet lightning across my brain.

I spread my arms wide, blinked, and gave her my loveliest, closed-mouth smile.

Peg caught her breath.

"I'm better," I said. "These are tears of happiness. I'm cured."

"But . . . oh, my Lord. . . ." Peg was stuttering.

"Mama did it," I said. "She laid her hands on me –"

"It's a miracle!" Peg shrieked. She picked me up and spun me around, or tried, anyway. She started to laugh and so did I, jubilant and thrilled.

Mama's voice cut through the noise.

"Peg? What are you thinking? You know I need the utmost quiet when I'm with a –"

"Oh, Missus!" sang Peg. "You've worked a miracle! Your little girl is cured!"

Mr. Poole stood next to Mama, staring at me, adjusting his glasses.

"Catherine? You did this?"

Mama's eyes locked with mine. I'm certain she was calculating her options. But I had her.

"You cured the girl?"

"Yes," she said, putting on a modest glow. "With help from the stars above, I have saved my precious daughter." She stretched out her hands, staring at them as if amazed by what they had done.

Peg squealed again and squeezed me. Mr. Poole squeezed Mama. Mama blushed, but she was watching me closely. I smiled. Deception runs in the family, after all. Mama taught me to lie. She should be proud of me.

"I'm tired," I said. Peg hustled me off to have a bath and go to bed, where she brought me supper on a tray. When Mama finally said good night to Mr. Poole and came in to see me, I was asleep. Faking sleep was nothing after faking daft.

Peg was a gossip marvel. Next morning, when I stepped outside with my hair brushed and my lips glossed, there must have been forty people waiting in line for Madame Caterina. Every one of them would be contributing to our house fund, and they all turned to look at me. And I was radiant.

Sammy Sanchez was leaning against the side of the building, skateboard rocking under his left foot.

"Hey," he said. "I heard about you."

"Yup," I said. "It's a miracle."

Road Trip

Martha Slaughter

I can't help it. I'm feeling a little mad at my grandpa, even though he's dead. I know it's so selfish of me, but, man! If Grandpa hadn't died I would *not* be sitting here in the backseat, behind my mother and my grandmother, driving a hundred million miles to Vermont, where we are going to visit Grammy's oldest friend. I'd be home hanging with my own friends.

Mom knows I didn't want to come. She said, "Evie, you can go to Border's and buy as many *Party Girls* books as you want, and you can buy yourself a Discman, too, and listen to lots of CD's."

Mom hates *Party Girls!*

She's been yelling at me the whole first part of the summer: "Why do you read that trash? Why can't you read a real book, Evie? I mean, those are just like watching television, they are so bad!"

And now she's handing me her credit card and telling me I can buy as many as I want.

She knows I do not want to be on this trip.

So I did go and buy the last *Party Girls* book, and there's another whole series called *Top Ten*, so I bought three of those, too. And a Discman with cool headphones.

Mom told me, "Stay up late the night before we go, and you can sleep most of the way there."

So I stayed up late, but when she woke me up the next morning I wanted to kill her. She was being so fussy and I wanted to scream. "Is this your suitcase? Did you remember a toothbrush? Did you bring something warm?"

And Grammy was clucking slightly – you know that little tongue click thing that grown-ups do. I could hear her.

She's been living with us since Grandpa died. I know she must be lonely. She tries to talk to me about rap music and IM, but what am I gonna say?

"She just sits at that computer all day," I heard her say to my mom.

"Well, that's what they do, Ma," says Mom.

Grammy thinks we should do things differently, I guess. Still, looking at her little gray head peeking up over the seat, well, I don't know. I'm sure she misses Grandpa.

Mom made a bed for me in the backseat. She put in a red blanket and her own special squishy pillow.

"Don't we need snacks?" says Grammy. "How can we go on a road trip with no snacks?"

"We'll stop along the way," says Mom.

"What, and pay three times as much?" says Grammy.

"It's okay, Ma," says Mom. "I'll pay."

I am already annoyed. I pull out *Party Girls* and put on my headphones as we head out of the driveway. This *Party Girls* is such a good one. I can't wait to gossip about it with Emily. She's read them all, and she's the one who told me about *Top Ten*.

"You're already that far, Evie?" Mom's voice echoes vaguely through my headphones.

"She's got her ears on," says Grammy. "She can't hear a thing."

I can hear through my headphones, but why let them know? I hear Grammy call them my ears, and it makes me smile. Slightly.

"What page are you on, Evie?" asks Mom.

"Eighty-seven."

"Already? Wow – and didn't you just start this morning?"

Mom is trying to connect with me. I can tell because she'll make a series of stupid comments. In a minute she'll reach her hand back and, unless I'm being the meanest person in the world, I'll give her what she wants – a little hand touch. I'm not much in the mood. Here's her hand. Fingertip brush only, no squeeze, but she'll take it.

Grammy is remembering her old friends. Do I care? Does Mom care? She is remembering friends named Verne and Gina. It's Gina we're going to see. I'm not listening, but sometimes I am. Verne had a sweet husband, who was Catholic and died very young. She had five kids. Gina's husband had a husky voice and was an alcoholic. Mom says, "Oh, I remember that voice and didn't Gina drink too much also?"

Grammy says she'll never forget the road trip she took with Gina. "Don't you remember?" she asks Mom. "It was you and me and Gina and her son, John. She would stop every half hour or so and go round to the trunk of the car to have a swig of gin. Do you remember at all?"

Mom says she sort of remembers the trip, but not

the gin swigs. "It's a wonder we weren't all killed!" says Mom, and Grammy agrees.

Grammy is remembering that this same Gina also traveled with a bottle of Lysol disinfectant in her purse. "Anywhere she stayed, she sprayed down the whole bathroom with Lysol."

I find myself wondering what in the world this woman looked like. A drunken germ freak. I can't picture it. But I don't want to ask because I don't want them to know I'm listening. I don't want to be a part of the conversation.

"Oh, there was a McDonald's!" says Grammy, as we speed by the rest stop.

Mom says, "Oh, Ma, did you want to stop?"

"No, no," says Grammy, "not unless you do."

"I would have been happy to stop. I'm sorry, Ma. We'll stop at the next one."

"Whatever you say," says Grammy.

Mom's hands get tight on the steering wheel. She says, "We'll stop at the next rest stop."

"Whatever you say," says Grammy.

Poor Grammy. She is trying to fit in and go with the flow, but I know she doesn't really even want to be swimming in this river.

After a while, we see the sign for the next rest stop.

"No McDonald's!" Grammy says.

"No, but there's a Burger King, Ma."

"Oh, I knew we should have stopped at that first one. I thought there would be a McDonald's at every rest stop! I just assumed."

She is disappointed, it seems to me, way deeper than McDonald's or Burger King deserves. I wish we had stopped at that McDonald's for her.

Although it's crazy that Grammy wants to stop at a McDonald's anyway. Grammy, of all people! She wouldn't have let Grandpa eat at McDonald's for anything. She spent every day of the last six months cooking healthy food that he hated. Every time we'd visit, that was all they talked about.

Too much fat in mayonnaise.

Too much salt in lunch meat.

Too much sugar in a baked potato!

"Well, I'm gonna stop," says Mom. "I like Burger King better than McDonald's anyway. Besides, I don't know about you guys, but I need to use the bathroom. Anybody else?"

Grammy shudders at the thought and I say no. But we go in to get some food.

"I'm going to the bathroom," says Mom. "You guys get me a Whopper with cheese. Take care of Grammy, Evie – don't lose her."

It's one of those huge bustling rest stops. There are hundreds of people looming at us from different directions. Poor little Grammy suddenly looks like a rowboat lost in a storm on the ocean. For a minute I see things through her eyes, and I hold on to her little arm.

"All these people, Evie," she says. "Where do they come from? And why are they all so big and fat?"

"I guess too many french fries," I say, and Grammy laughs. I squeeze her arm and together we work our way to the line. People are jostling us. I get a tray. It's a self-serve Burger King, so I grab a Whopper with cheese and fries for me, and the same for Mom.

"Don't they have one of those chicken sandwiches here, like they do at McDonald's?" says Grammy.

"Here's a chicken sandwich, Grammy."

"But that's a fried one – McDonald's has a grilled chicken sandwich. . . ."

I'm feeling the pressure of the line backing up behind us and I want to tell her to just take the crispy chicken so we can move along. I kind of want to yell at her.

"Oh, never mind," she says. "I'll just get some french fries and a hamburger." She sounds sad about this, but still I'm relieved.

"Wait! Oh, Grammy, here's what you want!" There does seem to be such a thing as a grilled chicken sandwich at Burger King after all. Her papery-soft face lights up. I can stop feeling bad about pushing the crispy chicken.

"Thank you, Evie," she says. "I'm sorry to be such a pain. I really haven't been out into the world for, well, really for years. Everything is different. Everything seems so confusing."

Poor Grammy! It drove me crazy, the way she fussed over Grandpa. But at least she knew what she was doing. At least she knew where everything was – her supermarket, her fruit store, the doctor's office, the hospital. It was hard to watch, the way she bustled up and down the stairs with food and medicines, always so worried, always with a turned-down mouth. But now, trying to help her figure out which size lid will fit on her plastic cup of Coke, I'm realizing how hard it must be for her. At least at home, even if they never had french fries, she knew where the salt and pepper and ketchup were.

"Oh, yum!" says Mom, back from the bathroom. "Should we sit and eat here, or in the car?"

"The car," says Grammy firmly.

And we're back on the road.

Grammy is remembering more about Grandpa. I'm wearing my ears, but I can still hear.

"I was such a small town girl," Grammy is saying.

"I'd never been anywhere until I went off to college. Grandpa was so romantic. When I was home in Maine after graduation one time, he told me to meet him at the Bangor airport. He got off the plane carrying a big bouquet of those pale orange roses, and he handed them to me and got back on the plane and went away."

Grandpa did that? Grandpa, who didn't leave his armchair as long as I can remember? I'm thinking how planes don't really turn around and fly back the way they came, but who knows! Maybe that's the way it was then.

"I was wearing a red button-down sweater," says Grammy. "I remember exactly the way this one tree looked – it had yellow leaves. You know how you have certain memories that last your whole life? I remember the sun shining and the wind blowing. It was the end of September, and in Maine it was already fall."

Mom sighs and says, "No wonder you married him."

Grammy snorts and says, "Oh, who knows? Maybe I'm remembering wrong. You know perfectly well Grandpa and I had our differences. Maybe I just wanted to get out of Maine."

"But still," says Mom.

"Yes, still," says Grammy.

And she starts to cry.

*

I start reading *Party Girls* again. Serena is buying a gray cashmere scarf at Barney's to give to Tim in her effort to lure him away from Blair, but I keep thinking of Grammy standing in her red sweater at the Bangor airport, with the sun shining and the wind blowing and Grandpa walking down the steps of the airplane with a big bouquet of pale orange roses. I know exactly the ones she likes. We get them for her every year, for her birthday, and she puts them on her front hall table.

"You were brave to marry Grandpa," says Mom. "I mean, you hadn't known each other that long. And you just married him, and moved to New York."

"Grandpa seemed so glamorous," says Grammy. "He was the kind of man who could get a table in a restaurant, no matter how crowded it was."

Mom asks Grammy, "Did you like living in New York?"

Grammy hates New York now. She never goes there. Never.

"Oh, yes, it was fun and exciting when I was first married. We lived in a little apartment on East 12th Street, with just a bed and an orange crate for a table. Once I tried to roast a chicken for dinner and, when he cut it, he said, "Do they always eat their chicken raw in Maine?"

I laugh out loud and Grammy turns around.

"What is it, Evie?" she says. "Is that book actually funny?"

I tell her no, that I like the story about the raw chicken. I can tell it makes her happy that I laughed at her story.

"How can that be true, Grammy?" I say. "You're the best cook ever."

It makes Mom happy, too, that I am joining in their conversation. The air in the car is all of a sudden lighter and easier to breathe.

"Well, I wasn't always," says Grammy. "Grandpa taught me how to cook."

"Oh, he didn't!" says Mom. "How can that be? He never cooked anything except bacon and eggs. He never did anything but cut the meat!"

"No, no, no," says Grammy. "In the beginning, he taught me how to cook."

It's a sunny day and Mom rolls down her window. The air pours in as we speed down the highway. For a while we can't talk because of the roaring sunny air. Grammy's soft silvery hair is shimmering across her cheek like the fine spray of a fountain. The scenery is a glistening green and there are darker mountains up ahead. I turn my music up loud. Grammy looks out the window at the streaking green countryside. She appears so forlorn that I feel a hot tear in the corner of my eye. I tap her shoulder. She reaches back without looking at me and we touch hands. Just like with Mom.

"Thank you, Evie," I can see her say.

And we all sink back into our silences – me with my music and my book, them with the roar of the open window, filling the empty spaces.

I finish my book. Grammy has fallen asleep, with her head back against the seat.

"Mom, are we anywhere near where we're going?" I say. I know I sound like a brat, but now that my book is done I remember that I am on a trip with my mother and my grandmother. We've been driving for hours and it looks like we're on the same endless highway we've been on the whole time.

"We are," says Mom. "We're almost in Burlington. Didn't you hear me say we were in Vermont?"

"No," I say. "I was reading my book. Is there gonna be TV in this hotel, Mom?"

"Evie," says Mom. "There is always TV in hotels."

Grammy is awake again. Mom tells her that she should take out the directions that Gina's daughter sent us to get to the hotel. Grammy rummages in her black canvas bag.

"I know I brought them," she says.

"You'll find them," says Mom.

"I put them in here," says Grammy. She starts pulling things out: her book on English gardens, her white toothbrush container, her leather wallet, a blue notebook with yellow Post-its poking out of every page. "I'm such a mess," she says. "I can't ever find anything. I'm so disorganized. . . ." Her voice is starting to shake.

I can tell Mom is irritated, but she's staying calm.

I don't want to be here. Why am I here? I want to be home. I want to be at Emily's. I want to be watching a movie on TV and prank phone-calling someone.

"I'm sure they're in there," says Mom.

I've seen my mom behave in the exact way that Grammy is now – a tornado of worry – but here Mom is, soothing her mother, saying she's sure she has the directions somewhere. And, of course, she does. She finds them, finally, at the bottom of the bag.

"Have we got to exit 7a yet?" asks Grammy.

"7a? On which road?"

"On route 4, going north."

"We're not on route 4, going north yet. We're still on the highway."

"Oh."

The conversation goes like this for several minutes.

Grammy starts turning her paper around, as if she can't read it. "The real problem is, I can't see a thing without my glasses. . . ."

"Where are your glasses?"

Grammy starts rummaging through her bag again.

"Grammy, what are those around your neck?" She's got one pair on her nose and another around her neck.

"Oh! I'm such a fool. Thank you, Evie, yes." She pulls the ones off her nose and jams on the others and starts reading the paper again. "I just can't quite tell. . . ."

"Ma," says Mom. "Give the paper to Evie – maybe she can tell where we are."

"No, no. I can see it now," says Grammy. "We should be looking for route 4. Route 4 and then exit 7a. That goes to route 22 and right into Burlington."

I lie down, on my back, with one leg crossed over the other. I turn my music up loud. I watch the tops of the trees whir by, and I think we will never get where we are going. For a minute I think I fall asleep and, when I wake up, I can see that evening is coming.

*

Grammy is talking about Gina again.

"After all, it was her ex-husband, Tom, who introduced me to Grandpa in the first place," she says.

"I was always scared of Tom," says Mom.

"So was I!" says Grammy. "I don't know if I would have gotten married if I hadn't been so scared of him. I couldn't decide; Grandpa was ten years older. My family didn't want me to marry him at all. But Gina's husband told me, 'I've canceled my appointments today. Either get married, or call it off.'"

I'm still lying down with my headphones on. But I've turned the music off.

"I didn't know your family didn't want you to marry him," says Mom.

"Well, he was so wild," says Grammy. "He took me places that my family would never go. Nightclubs and restaurants – he even took me to a prizefight."

"Well, you stood up to them, didn't you?" says Mom.

"Did I?" says Grammy. "Or was it just that Tom Hambly canceled his appointments that day?"

"But the roses!"

"Yes, I know," says Grammy. "Grandpa turned out to be a wonderful person, he really did. My mother always said how she ended up liking him a lot better than she liked me." And her face crumples, again.

"Oh, Mom, there's a sign for route 4!"

"Oh, good work, Evie," says Mom.

"Well, thank heaven *someone* can see in this group!" says Grammy, sniffing and laughing.

It seems like forever until we get to exit 7a, which is route 22 to Burlington. Dusk has settled in, and the mountains are black against a lavender sky.

"What's the name of the street the hotel is on?" Mom asks Grammy, who's still clutching the directions.

"Hopkins Street," says Grammy. "It says. . . ."

Hopkins Street is a long bright street, on the edge of Lake Champlain. I know Mom found a hotel with a view of the lake because she thought it would be nice for Grammy. I know she chose the most expensive hotel because she thought it would have the cleanest bathrooms.

"It seems like the kind of thing Grandpa would do," she told me, while she was on hold for the reservation.

"Look for the Westwood Hotel," she says to us now.

"Goodness," says Grammy. "So many people."

"I see it, Mom!" I shout. "Right up ahead, on the corner there."

The Westwood Hotel has a thousand windows gleaming with the reflection of the wide silvery water of Lake Champlain. I sense it is not what Grammy was hoping for. She is sinking in her seat and the atmosphere of our car shifts, from excitement to a slight dread.

I know Mom has to feel it – the dread coming from her own mother – but she's ignoring it. She's looking for the parking.

"Over there, Mom," I say. "See? It's one of those underground garages."

The dread thickens.

"Underground garage?" says Grammy.

"It's not a big deal, Ma," says Mom. "Haven't you ever been in one of those underground garages, at the airport or someplace?"

Mom knows perfectly well that Grammy has never been in an underground garage. Grammy lives in her green garden and her sun-filled house, in an overlit supermarket or a fluorescent hospital room, in her flowery upstairs bedroom and her old book-lined library. She has never, ever, been underground – except to check for leaks in her own basement.

Mom turns into the garage and drives slowly down the ramp. Grammy is breathing in a shallow way and holding her bag in her lap.

"Like entering the gates of hell, right, Ma?" says my mom, lightly. "Except it's just a parking garage."

Grammy smiles and forces a small laugh. I've been in a million underground parking garages and never thought twice about it. But somehow, driving down with Grammy, it does seem kind of creepy, going down and down in a tight circle.

"Here, Mom. 'PARKING AVAILABLE'," I say. "LEVEL 3."

We turn slowly onto level 3. The concrete ceiling feels too low and the pillars are rough and thick. We all sit for a minute in the car, not quite ready to brave this dark close place we find ourselves in.

"Okay, come on," says Mom, cheerfully. "We just have to find the elevator."

"Elevator?" says Grammy.

I feel a little sorry for Mom. She meant so well, taking Grammy to the nicest hotel she could find. And now here we are in an underground parking garage with a person who is revealing she's not keen on elevators, either. It's like we lost our way along the sunny path we were traveling, and somehow found ourselves in the thick of the forest.

"Come on, Grammy," I say. "Elevators aren't so bad. They're quick."

We get out of the car. The scenery is too grim for Mom to even try to cheer Grammy up. Without speaking, we herd my small, withering grandmother into the elevator and push the button for LOBBY.

"Finally!" says Mom, ten seconds later when the doors open. We have to wind our way past a glittering fountain and blazing chandeliers to get to the front desk. Grammy is shrinking in front of my eyes. My mother, on the other hand, is looking taller than usual.

"Evie, why don't you and Grammy sit right there while I check in?" she says, in a hard voice.

Grammy and I sit on some fat chairs, with maroon-and-green striped upholstery.

"I'm sorry, Evie," she says to me, softly. "It's all so overwhelming, the garage and the lights. I haven't been anywhere in so very long."

I am torn between sympathy for her and sympathy for my mother. I wish that I was at home, sitting at the computer, or meeting my friends at Cosimo's for pizza. I wish, at least, I had my headphones on, with my music as loud as it goes.

"It's okay, Grammy," I say, and I pat her soft hand. "It'll be okay."

Mom comes back, still looking tall and tight. But when she sees her mother, she softens. "Okay, Ma," she says. "I got the keys. One more elevator and we'll be safe in our room." Grammy and I slide off the fat striped chairs and follow Mom.

None of us are talking. I'm mad about not being in a booth at Cosimo's; Mom is disappointed because her plan for making Grammy happy is not working; and Grammy is just sad and frightened, wishing with all her heart to have her old life back, which is gone forever.

We get out of the elevator into a long hallway, with doors going in both directions. The floor is carpeted in red-and-gold swirls and the walls are papered in a silver flower pattern.

"This way," says Mom. She has given up trying to be cheerful. "I got two rooms so Evie can watch her own TV, but there's a connecting door so we can feel like we're all together."

She opens the door and we stand there, faced with big brown furniture. Mom puts her bag on one of the beds and opens the door to the next room.

"Here we go," she says. She knows she has lost the war, but she seems willing to fight the battle through to the end. Grammy follows her in and puts her suitcase down. Mom pulls open the curtains. We stare at the view; the sky is purple and quilted, the lake a dark shimmer.

I feel relieved that we all know where we stand. It is clear that Grammy is not ready to face the world, even with lake views and expensive hotel rooms. Our mission has been reduced to getting through the next day until we can turn around and go home. It's as if

Grammy has revealed herself as disabled and now we simply need to protect her until she is back in a safe environment. There is no real point in trying to make her happy.

Grammy walks over and peers in the bathroom. "Oops, I forgot my Lysol," she says, and we all laugh together.

"Let's have dinner in the restaurant here," says Mom. "I doubt the food will be good, but at least it's right here." Grammy and I say that's fine.

It's hard to explain why we have such a peaceful dinner, after a day with so much upheaval. I know Mom had higher hopes for this trip, and I am guessing that Grammy did, too, or she wouldn't have been willing to come.

I didn't want to be here at all, but I think I'm glad that I came. It's like, with our three different paces, we tried to climb a mountain that was too hard to climb. We never made it to the top, but along the way we found a place where we could be together.

This restaurant at the Westwood Hotel, in Burlington, Vermont, feels like a small green meadow on the harsh side of a cold gray mountain.

That night, late, when I am watching TV and Mom is sleeping, I hear Grammy crying in the other room. I tiptoe over and slide in next to her. I hold on to her tightly while she cries and cries and cries.

After a while, she stops.

"I'm sorry, Evie," she says. "I was trying to turn on the TV to watch the food channel, like I did with Grandpa, but I couldn't figure out how to do it. Isn't that silly? It was the remote control that made me cry so hard. That stupid thing made me realize that Grandpa is really gone."

"Oh, Grammy," I say. I'm pretty sure neither of us is tired. "Shall we see what's on the food channel?" I turn it on and together we watch.

"On the way home, Grammy," I say, holding her small velvet hand, "we'll stop at McDonald's. On the way home, we'll get the right kind of chicken sandwich."

Grammy laughs. "You know what, Evie?" she says. "I'm looking forward to that."

Meet the Authors

Susan Adach

Susan was bitten by the writing bug in grade five, when she won the prize for English composition. She now works for the premier of Ontario, helping with his speeches. At night, she writes stories about mitten hunters, the true story of the cow jumping over the moon, or the story of a boy whose brother disappears under the bed. She lives in a teeny house in Toronto with her family: husband, Richard, daughter, Jessica, and cat, Merry.

One of Susan's favorite books was *Gidget* by Frederick Kohner.

Anne Laurel Carter

Anne left Don Mills, when she was seventeen, to travel and work in other countries. She returned to Canada to become a teacher and has taught in Northern Quebec and Southern Ontario. While horses often find a way into her stories (*Under a Prairie Sky, My*

Home Bay, Last Chance Bay), she's still hoping to learn how to ride bareback in the circus ring.

One of Anne's favorite books was *Mara, Daughter of the Nile* by Eloise McGraw.

Gillian Chan

Gillian was born in England. Because her father was an officer with the Royal Air Force, the family moved every two years. This led to Gillian being a good observer, a useful characteristic in a writer. Gillian taught high school before becoming a full-time author. She has written short stories for adults as well as for kids, and several children's novels, including the prize-winning *The Carved Box* and *A Foreign Field*, and, most recently, *The Turning*. She lives with her husband and her son.

One of Gillian's favorite books was *The Chrysalids* by John Wyndham.

Anne Gray

Anne was born in Mobile, Alabama, the youngest of four siblings. Between chores, her mother says Anne always had her nose in a book. She has had other stories published in magazines, but *Uncle Cory's Smile* is the first one in a book. Now she is married and lives in Hamilton, Ontario, where she's completing her first fantasy novel for teenagers.

One of Anne's favorite books was *Lad: A Dog* by Albert Payson Terhune.

Nancy Hartry

Nancy is the author of two picture books: *Hold On, McGinty!* and *Jocelyn and the Ballerina.* She is always stealing story ideas from her kids, her family, and complete strangers in restaurants. She wears mirrored sunglasses and carries a notebook wherever she goes. When she is not writing stories, she works as a lawyer. During her breaks, she spies on the people in the park and makes up stories about them. Watch out. You could be next.

One of Nancy's favorite books was *A Wrinkle in Time* by Madeleine L'Engle.

Marthe Jocelyn

Marthe grew up in the east end of Toronto, known as The Beaches. With her sister and two brothers, she often put on plays or circuses in the backyard. She loved to read and organized a lending library, using her own books, each with a hand-printed library card. As she got older, Marthe had many different jobs, including waitress, sailor, and toy designer before finally publishing her first book, *The Invisible Day*, when she was forty. Since then, she has written eleven books, some of which she also illustrated. Marthe's husband, Tom Slaughter, is an artist too. They have two daughters, Hannah and Nell, and a cat named Moe, who thinks she's a dog.

One of Marthe's favorite books was *The Borrowers* by Mary Norton.

Julie Johnston

Julie was born in Smiths Falls, Ontario. Since high school, she has been writing short stories, magazine articles, plays, and novels. Her work, including *The Only Outcast* and *In Spite of Killer Bees*, has won many awards. Her most recent book, *Susanna's Quill*, was published in the fall of 2004. She now writes full-time, both in Peterborough, where she lives with her husband, and at their cottage on Big Rideau Lake, where she spends her summers. Julie and her husband have four daughters and seven grandchildren.

One of Julie's favorite books was *Anne of the Island* by Lucy Maud Montgomery.

Dayal Kaur Khalsa

Dayal Kaur Khalsa was born in Queens, New York. She traveled for many years before settling in Canada, where she wrote and illustrated stories about her childhood: her love for her gambling grandmother; her desire for a pet dog; the wonderful day she discovered pizza. Dayal Kaur Khalsa wrote and illustrated eight books in the three years before her death (in 1989), each life-affirming work created while she was seriously ill. Her legacy – *Tales of a Gambling Grandma*, *I Want a Dog*, *How Pizza Came to Our Town*, *Sleepers*, *My Family Vacation*, *Cowboy Dreams*, *Julian*, and *The Snow Cat* – is an outstanding testament to a brave and talented artist.

Loris Lesynski

While creating her most recent book of verse, *Zigzag: Zoems for Zindergarten*, Loris Lesynski had to spend so many hours in rambunctious kindergartens that writing for old people in middle school makes a welcome change. Loris is also the author and illustrator of many picture books and poetry collections, starting with the curiously popular *Boy Soup* and including *Dirty Dog Boogie*, *Nothing Beats a Pizza*, and *Cabbagehead*. She's currently at work on a middle-grade novel called *The Nevers*.

One of Loris's favorite books was *A Tree Grows in Brooklyn* by Betty Smith.

Martha Slaughter

Martha grew up in Pennsylvania with two sisters and two dogs. In the eighth grade, she wrote a play called *Symmetry*, which her classmates performed at the end of the year. She is now the publisher of a literary magazine called *Gumbo*. She has three children – Sam, Joe, and Willa – and a pesky dog named Lizzy. Although she has written dozens of stories for adults, *Road Trip* is her first one for children.

One of Martha's favorite books was *The Song of the Lark* by Willa Cather.

Teresa Toten

Like most kids, Teresa grew up in a house bursting with secrets. Unfortunately, they usually burst out of Teresa too, along with a lot of extra bits to make them "even more interesting." Apparently, this was a bad thing. Teresa kept getting into trouble over spilt secrets until someone explained that if you write them down and call them a story, you're considered a writer. Apparently, this was a good thing. Her first two books of secrets are *The Onlyhouse* and *The Game*. Teresa's first picture book is called *Bright Red Kisses* and it's full of kisses, not secrets.

One of Teresa's favorite books was *The Sword in the Stone* by T.H. White.

Elizabeth Winthrop

Elizabeth Winthrop is the author of over fifty books for children and adults, including *Island of Justice*, *The Castle in the Attic*, *Dumpy LaRue*, and *Dog Show*. Her short stories have been collected in various anthologies including *Best American Short Stories* and have twice won the PEN Syndicated Fiction Award. Among her many honors, she has won a number of state book awards for her middle-grade fiction.

One of Elizabeth's favorite books was *The Member of the Wedding* by Carson McCullers.